Changes

In

Life

Changes in Life

Copyright © 2014 KC Riley-Gyer

Please note the author is Australian. Therefore, all spelling, grammar and punctuation will be Australian based.

This is a work of fiction. While based in a real location, any reference to anything real is a coincidence. All brand names belong to their maker.

National Library of Australia Cataloguing-in-Publication entry

Author: Riley-Gyer, KC, author.
Title: Changes in Life / KC Riley-Gyer.
ISBN: 9780992467708 (paperback)
Subjects: Shapeshifting--Fiction. Fantasy fiction.
Dewey Number: A823.4

Published with the assistance of www.inhousepublishing.com.au

Changes
In Life

KC Riley-Gyer

Also by KC Riley-Gyer

The Unnaturals of Brisbane Series

Objective: The Crimson Empire

Changes in Degrees

Acknowledgements

Doug is awesome. LOL Despite him teasing me by typing that, yes he is. When it comes to my writing he is ever so patient even when I frustrate the hell out of him.

I would also like to thank a certain group of fishies from a particular pond that doesn't exist anymore. Without them and their stories, this series may never have gotten off the ground like it did. Fishie fin hugs to you all.

Back when I wrote the first draft in 2009, there had been a mention that Tom Clancy's Rainbow Six was going to be made into a movie. I loved the idea (and still do) so I wrote a scene mentioning it as a completed movie. Six or more months later, information about that movie disappeared. However, because this is a work of fiction, I decided to leave the movie reference in.

Chapter 1

"Life isn't stagnant, never has been and never will be. After 25 years, one would think I would be used to changes, but it's like someone keeps throwing road blocks in my way. Sometimes I am able to see them in time, others I crash into them in a big way. In all things, life changes, whether we like it or not." – Sarah.

"Just when one thinks things are going the way one wants them to, something happens and changes the way one looks at, and deals with, things. I guess my choice of lifestyle became the framework for how I react to situations I find myself in; and this is no different. No matter what path one chooses, changes always happen, these changes affect one's choices and thus one's sense of justice." – Kaelan.

~*~

It had been four hours since he had walked out of her life for the second time since she'd met him. Two days ago, when she woke up, she had thought the New Year was off to a good start.

1

Today she didn't want to know about it. There were still almost eleven months left. She hoped it would improve as time went by, but doubted it would. Not now.

Having had next to no sleep during the past two days, since he had told her the hit was a go, she sat at his kitchen table, in his house and she was stuck there. He had all her stuff packed and moved to his house, and the apartment she used to rent was now occupied by someone else. It was still too emotional for her to even think about the house Brandi and Abel had left her in their will; let alone actually go to it. Not only that, but he had set up a new building on his property just for her... Her very own nail bar home business.

'Damn it, but I have to admit that he did a wonderful job in setting it all up with its own driveway and little car park. At first, I had thought he had just organised its construction, but I saw him working with the other men. Some of whom I recognised; like Scott and Zac. Who could have foreseen this latest particular problem of mine when agreeing to stay in his house.'

Deciding life must go on, she had dragged herself out of bed since she couldn't sleep. Sitting in her usual spot at the table she stared out the window looking at the bushland and the rain, which was a constant drizzle with everything looking grey. The weather suited her mood; miserable and bleak. With her hands wrapped around her cup of tea, she was building up the courage to pick up the phone to call Antonio. She had to do it. She had no choice.

Neither she nor Kaelan had known that the rogue hunters, who had murdered her friends and had attempted to kill her at the end of October last year, had had a therian with them. As a result, neither she nor Kaelan had been armed with silver ammunition when the therian had attacked her. Only him being well armed, had used a shotgun to blow the therian to smithereens, had prevented her from dying.

Since she was back in his house, he obviously succeeded. To a point. There was less than two weeks to go till the next full moon and that didn't leave much time to learn things before the first change. She sighed, knowing she couldn't put it off any longer, stood up and headed into the kitchen. Rinsing her cup out, she then grabbed the phone and called Antonio.

"Hello, Antonio here." A chirpy Italian male voice answered.

"Hi Antonio. It's Sarah." She greeted hesitantly.

"SARAH! Shit Luv where the hell have you been...?"

"I..." She didn't get the chance to say anything more.

"...No one has heard from you in almost three months. We thought you died in that fire at Danny's place..."

"An..."

"...You are an inconsiderate cow. You know that don't you?" He interrupted with a comment only a friend could get away with.

"ANTONIO!" She shouted in exasperation.

"WHAT?!"

"I'm a therian and need your help." She responded quietly.

"Oh Luv, I'm sorry, but you had us worried you know." Antonio suddenly sounded upset instead of angry.

"I'm sorry. The past three and a half months haven't been the best for me either and it's a very, very long story. This is my address in Gumdale... Are you able to come over?"

"You sound horrid Luv. Sure, I can come over. What flavour are you?"

She sighed softly. "I'm okay, and jaguar."

"Well, shit. They're rare out of the Americas. I didn't even know there were any here at all. I'll do a bit of research and see what info within Australia I can find out for you Luv. Despite the fact that he's the head of the leopards, I'm going to bring Jonathon with me since he's also the chairman of the league. He might have some ideas as to how to help you since jaguars are similar to leopards. See you soon okay?"

"Okay, till then."

They hung up.

The day had just started and already she was tired; and not just from a lack of sleep. She just wanted to crawl into a hole and never come back out. However, she knew that would never happen. She sighed. The next chore for the day was to talk to Mick and Toby, but before that happened she needed another cuppa. So, she concentrated on making it instead of thinking about anything else.

She went back into the kitchen and grabbed her cup, placed a Twinings English Breakfast tea bag in it – she was too lazy to make up a pot of tea just then and opted for the easy way out. She walked over to the eight litre electric urn that was on 24/7 and three quarter filled her cup from it. After dunking the tea bag for the desired time, she removed it, scooped in three teaspoons of sugar...

'Hey... I'm a crabby ole cow and need all the sweetening I can get.' She thought to herself. It was a regular teasing comment she made about herself whenever someone mentioned her sugar intake.

...then poured a generous amount of pure cream into her cup and stirred until she was satisfied that all the sugar was dissolved. Then it occurred to her, now that she was a therian she could have cream any time she wanted.

'Huh. Here's to finding an upside to this fudging situation.'

Taking a sip, it was good. She had just sat down at the table when the guys came back from shopping. They paused as they came in when they saw her but she didn't say a word. She waited until they did.

"Morning." They both greeted at the same time and both sounded like they were walking on egg shells as they continued into the kitchen and put the groceries away.

"Morning guys." She responded softly as she held her tea. She watched them.

"How are you feeling?" Toby asked. Mick shook his head slightly as if he thought it was the wrong question to ask.

Sarah couldn't help a small smile as she took another sip of her tea. "I've been better, but... all in all... I'm okay I guess."

Once the groceries had been put away and they had their coffees, they sat at the table. She put her cup down but still had her hands wrapped around it.

"We need to talk." She stated as she gazed at them.

They glanced at each other then back at her. "Okay." Toby said.

"First, what do you think you know about what happened to me since... Kaelan... and I left to do the hit?" She had a difficult time saying his name without choking on it because of her feelings for him and more than likely never seeing him again.

"We know you were hurt, but Kaelan didn't say how or in what way you were hurt. To be honest, you don't look too badly hurt from what Toby had told me." Mick said.

"And we know you love him." Toby said sort of flatly.

'Well, I guess that covers it and Toby seems upset over something. Oh well, one problem at a time.'

"Kaelan left just after three this morning and won't be back till goodness knows when, if at all. No matter what, you can't tell him how I feel about him. Even if he asks. It's my life, for better or worse and it's something he and I have to deal with, without help from anyone else." She paused, opened her mouth but nothing came out so she closed it. She took another sip then tried again.

"There was a woman there, but there had been no intel on her other than she wasn't a vampire. She turned out to be a therian. She attacked me, so badly that I should have died." She paused again, looking down at the cup in her hands. They waited for her to continue.

"I healed about three days of injuries in just under twenty-four hours." Sarah watched their shock as they realised what she was saying. "I am now a were-jaguar."

She let the information sink in for a minute or two before resuming. "I'm no longer human. If you want to leave I won't hold it against either of you."

"You might not but I think he will." Toby said. She was grateful that he didn't say the name.

"He's not here anymore so he has no right to get upset about anything that happens here. This is between the three of us. He's no longer part of the equation." She informed as her voice caught slightly in her throat.

"Easy to say, Girl, but you love him and that isn't as easy." Mick stated as he gazed at her intently.

She sighed. "Yeah, I know, but I can only do the best I can. While he isn't here I have to keep him out of the equation for my own emotional well being." She said quietly. "So, I am giving you both the choice to leave if you wish to. Things have changed so much since Danny's death..."

"How can you love him if you were supposed to be in love with Danny?" Toby frowned at her.

'And there's his problem. Even though I thought Mick would be the one with the problem over this situation.' Sarah mentally sighed. 'I so do not need this right now.'

However, she decided to clear the subject once and for all.

"I was only attracted to Danny. Me loving him was hindered by a number of things... one: The death of my husband, two: My shyness, and three: I met and was strongly attracted to... Kaelan... long before I met Danny. I was conflicted between the two of them. I didn't know if I loved him more than... Kaelan or not.

"I didn't want to hurt Danny, that's the other reason why I didn't just grab at what he was offering. I'm not that sort of woman. Our friendship grew to an attraction, and if he hadn't been killed then it very well may have turned into love between us. I don't know. However, things didn't work out that way, and not just because of Kaelan." Her eyes started welling with tears and she savagely wiped them away.

"I'm sorry Sarah." Toby apologised quietly and sincerely.

She shook her head as she looked out the window trying to stop crying. "I just want to know if you want to cut your losses and leave or not." She whispered.

Toby reached for her hand, while Mick stood up, came around to her and hugged her from behind. Mick moved his head so he was looking at Toby.

"We're staying if that's okay with you." Toby said.

Sarah cried and they just held her. 'I really need to get my shit together.'

An hour later Antonio and Jonathon arrived. As per usual, before she was rescued by Kaelan, she had the stereo playing softly in the background from the lounge room. She was vaguely aware of it being on as she escorted them into the kitchen. Earlier, she'd asked Toby and Mick if they would make themselves scarce for a little while and, to her relief, they went out.

"Hello Jonathon, Antonio. Would you like something to eat or drink?" While Antonio and Sarah were friends and she had met Jonathon before, she didn't know Jonathon all that well.

Both Jonathon and Antonio were taller than her, but that was where the similarities ended. Jonathon was African dark to Antonio's Italian olive. Antonio had short wavy dark brown hair to Jonathon's black short-short tightly curly hair. Jonathon had a tall slim athletic build to Antonio's slightly shorter broader – not as in excess weight but just not lithe – build. Antonio's happy-go-lucky attitude to Jonathon's more serious and formal one. Jonathon preferred to be called Jonathon, while Antonio will answer to Antonio, Ant, Tonio and Tony. Antonio was younger than Jonathon.

"Nothing for me, thank you." Jonathan declined in his very formal voice.

"Coffee please Luv. But geez you look like shit." Antonio was his usual self of blunt, teasing and cheerful.

"Such the charmer Ant." She retorted sarcastically and rolled her eyes at him.

She had basically forgotten she had the stereo on until a particular song started playing...

...the roof, the roof is on fire.

The roof, the roof, the roof is on fire.

"Sorry. Let me rephrase that... Love the new body, but you do look like shit."

With a raised eyebrow she handed him his coffee. "Keep digging Ant. You haven't reached the core yet but you're getting there real fast."

Jonathon snorted in amusement at her comment. "How long have you been a therian and how many changes have you been through?" He asked suddenly serious.

We don't need no water

let the motherfucker burn.

Burn motherfucker burn.

Suddenly, Jonathon snorted again and rolled his eyes. While Antonio burst out laughing and almost sprayed a mouthful of coffee. He had just managing to swallow it before he laughed with a couple of coughs, and asked about the song.

"Blood Hound Gang's *'The Roof is on Fire'*." Blushing as she told them, then answered Jonathon's original question.

"None, I became therian around sunset the night before last." With that she revealed her lower torso, showing the still vivid but healing claw marks. "She got me from left shoulder down to just above the navel then just below it and down across the right thigh. She also gnawed my right shoulder. I was told I that I had started healing on the operating table and was mostly healed in twenty-four hours."

Antonio whistled long and low. Whether he was impressed with the description of the injury, the healing rate or both, she didn't know.

"And the therian who attacked you?" Jonathon asked.

"She was killed in the attempt to save my life. The men she was with had had a legal hit taken out against them. They were the ones who had killed Danny and two of my friends." She took a deep breath then let it out. "Let me start at the beginning..."

The really short version, as in just the basics, had only taken a couple of minutes to tell. Even after three and a half months, it was still too emotional for her to go into the full details. The short version kept the tears at bay.

"You're extremely lucky you didn't die." Antonio commented, sounding impressed.

"Yeah. I had a very determined friend who kept me alive. Both times." She said quietly.

"An exceptionally good friend then." Jonathon commented. His tone was one of control as if he was conducting a business deal instead of being involved in people's lives.

"Yeah." She responded softly.

"With no Jaguars in Australia, one of my Leopards will train you." Jonathon stated bluntly and with little emotion.

She nodded.

"Sarah, I understand you have been through a lot, but now you must go through a lot more for a few more months. As to how long will depend on your own personal strengths. From what I have seen of you, you are what we classify as a lesser pack member. You are not a dominating person. Others will be able to dominate you and there will be nothing you can do about it because you aren't strong enough.

"So, it could be up to a year or more of training before you are deemed safe to be around during the moon's major influences. Strength isn't just power or physical. With therians it is both, as well as something else and that something else is something that determines where in the hierarchy you'll stand. We... don't exactly know what it is. All we do know is it is part of the therianthropy disease and that it eventually makes itself known, to whatever degree, within the person it resides." Jonathon stated.

She nodded, looking at Jonathon, then Antonio. However, something in Antonio's expression suggested there was something he didn't agree with what Jonathon had said. Admittedly, to herself, she too didn't like Jonathon's assessment of her but suspected he was right. Although, that didn't mean she had to like it.

"Since you seem comfortable with Antonio, he'll be your chaperon and educator until we deem you safe to be with unaltereds at the time of full moon. Although, it is highly recommended that therians stay away from their unaltered family during that time. Antonio will answer any questions and help you with any problems you might have." Jonathon stood up. "Something like this is a mixed blessing. While it isn't something you wanted, welcome to the family Sarah."

"Thank you Jonathon." She saw him out and he left since the two men had arrived in their own cars. She stood there watching his car as it disappeared from sight and heard Antonio come up behind her as she leant against the door jamb.

"I can hear things I never could before." She murmured without turning around.

Antonio wrapped his arms around her shoulders and she straightened up. "Part and parcel of what we are Luv." He hugged her. "I'm sorry this happened to you and that you're having a hard time. I'll help you as much as I possibly can, but I can't guarantee that it'll be smooth and painless." He said softly, leaning his chin on the top of her head.

"Thank you and I know. Very little has gone smooth and painless for me, ever." His arms tightened slightly in a hug.

"While I know we heal amazingly fast and start losing weight at a faster pace than usual once we become therian, I know you didn't lose all that excess weight overnight."

"I spent the past three and a half months here exercising it off."

"Ah. Why so sad Luv?" He asked gently.

She paused, then realised she had to talk to someone and, out of everyone still around her, Antonio was probably the closest to her now. She also knew that by revealing those details she could lose his friendship. With a need she hadn't realised was there, she took the risk.

"The man who owns this house saved my life the night Danny died. I was told he fought hard to keep me alive, I'd met him a couple of years before that. Anyway, he helped me exercise and trained me in weapon use because I'd asked him to. I wanted revenge and I knew a legal hit would eventually be taken out on the killers. So, by joining him on the hunt I could have my revenge without being charged with murder. Pre-meditated, I know. Anyway, I fell in love with him. Hard. I'm not sure but I think he might have felt the same way."

"You don't think he does now?"

Just like that, there was no accusation in his voice. It surprised her that he accepted what she had just said without complaint or surprise of any kind.

"Before I answer that... Aren't you horrified at what I'd just said?"

"No Luv. What they did was wrong and I'm glad they got their just desserts. I'm just surprised you willingly volunteered to do such a thing. Now, why do you think he doesn't love you any more?"

His acceptance surprised her so she just let the subject be and continued with the flow of the discussion. In that moment, she knew she had a permanent friend in Antonio.

"I've become one of the monsters he loves to hunt, Tony. So no, I don't think he does any more. I don't even know if we're still friends." She answered then thought. 'If he even loved me in the first place; if we were even friends in the first place.' The tears started flowing again. Even though she didn't make a sound he hugged her tighter. She suspected a tear or two might have fallen on his arms.

"Well, he'll be back. You're in his house after all."

"I'm not so sure about that. This house has spent a lot of its time empty apparently. That's why he offered to let me stay here cheaply, plus he added a building on the property here for me to work from home in. If I were to see him again it would more than likely be to fulfil a promise." She answered sadly.

"I see." He paused. "Are you back at work yet?"

"No. That's my next chore, start calling past clients to see if they want to come back."

"Don't. At least not yet. I want you to not work for the next month at least. You might be fine during this coming week, but the last few days leading to the full moon might find you in a situation or two that you won't be able to handle. Would you be okay if Maria and I stayed here with you? When there's only one new therian we tend to work in tandem. When there's more than one, she chaperons the guy if there is one."

"Okay, I see, I won't work then. Not a problem for both you

and Maria to stay here. I would like that very much, actually. I have Mick and Toby here as well. When will I be able to start work again? I'm going to need money coming in soon to pay the bills."

'He would have a fit if he knew they would be staying here.' Then she pushed the unexpected thought away. 'Well, tough. He's not here now and I need the support of my friends since he's deserted me.' She fought a fresh round of tears.

"Hmmm... make it... after your second full moon. I know that's a long time to have no money coming in but Maria and I will help out while we stay here. Get Toby and Mick to help out financially as well for the duration at least."

She just nodded.

Suddenly Antonio unwrapped himself from her then answered his mobile that starting playing David Bowie's *'Putting Out The Fire With Gasoline'* in his pants' pocket. "Hey my little Hellcat. What you up to...? Ahh okay. How would you like to pack some stuff for us for at least a three week stay with Sarah?"

Sarah then realised it was Maria.

"SHE'S ALIVE?!" Sarah suddenly heard her shrieking from his phone and couldn't help smiling. Only, the smile didn't last long. She was starting to feel battered and worn.

Antonio winced, pulling the phone away from his ear briefly, "Yeah, long story which we will tell you when you get here..." He stared at the phone then gazed incredulously at Sarah. "She hung up. I think we can expect her here in less than an hour. Just hope she doesn't get a speeding ticket. One moment while I message her the address" Antonio laughed.

Sarah gave a weary smile and headed back into the kitchen to make a fresh cuppa. She held up Antonio's cup to see if he wanted another and he said yes, so she put his cup on the bench then pointed out where the coffee, sugar, milk, hot water and teaspoons were with a slightly cheeky smile on her face. He laughed and rolled his eyes and made himself a cuppa as well once he had finished on the mobile.

"If you're going to be staying here then you need to know where everything is so you can make it yourself." She chuckled at him.

"No, you're the probie so it's your job to make it for me." He exclaimed in mock seriousness.

Sarah laughed throwing the tea-towel at him. "You and your NCIS. One of your nicks may be Tony but your last name isn't DiNozzo. Start that probie business and I'll tell Maria." She said in a mock threat but she was still smiling too much for it to be taken seriously.

Antonio clutched at his heart dramatically. "You wouldn't?! Oh... You would! You meanie you." He laughed then hugged her when she rolled her eyes at him. "Feeling better?"

"Yes and thank you." She smiled at him.

After she finished her cup of tea, she stood up. "I'm going to put my things into the master bedroom so you and Maria can have the room I've been using."

"We could take another room Luv. Don't want to displace you."

"You're not. The master bedroom is the only other room vacant so I was already planning to move my things into it today anyway."

"Okay then." Antonio responded.

So Sarah tackled a job she wasn't really looking forward to. But by having to do it right then prevented her from dragging out the inevitable. With her injuries still hurting her, she moved slowly but consistently.

By the time Maria arrived, Sarah had everything moved and the bed remade with fresh sheets for them. By the time everything was done she was glad of the other woman's arrival to distract her from the memories in his room.

During the move she found her mobile phone at the back of the bottom drawer of the tallboy. It looked a little melted around the edges. She checked it to see if it still worked but it didn't. So she phoned the mobile service she used to see if the account and number were still active. After confirmation, she was thankful they were. Because she used a pre-paid service she had to make sure she hadn't gone over the expiry date of the sim card – due to not recharging the phone credit – or she would have lost ownership of the number.

She told them she needed a new phone and sim card because they had been damaged in an accident and had only just found the phone. They sent her an email outlining the handsets they had in store. She checked them out while they spoke so she could order and pay for it right there via their website. While looking, she decided to order accessories for her new smartphone. When they told her she would get it the next day by express courier at no extra cost to her, she was pleased at having spent so much. She happily thanked them then hung up.

After finishing organising a new mobile phone, it reminded

her about her scooter. 'Well, damn... I'll have to talk to Mick and Toby about it. I hadn't thought about it during my recuperation at all.'

Chapter 2

As soon as Maria walked through the door she started going mad at Sarah while hugging her to within a millimetre…

'Lot smaller than an inch obviously.' Sarah mused.

…of her life. Antonio laughed and disengaged his wife from her. Sarah then spent the next half hour showing Maria the bedroom, bathroom then back to the kitchen for a cuppa to fill her in on the past three and a half months of Sarah's life.

When one listens to Maria, before seeing her, one envisions an open motherly plump Italian. Instead she's fractionally taller than Sarah and slimmer than her, even in Sarah's current state of weight loss. Maria's hair was such a dark brown it was almost black and cut in a very stylish short style. She had an olive complexion, beautiful sparkling brown eyes and a ready smile.

"Such a difficult time for you Honey." She then turned to Antonio as the three of them sat in the lounge room; them on the lounge and Sarah in a matching chair beside Maria. "I take it you haven't really discussed anything with her yet?"

"Not until you got here. I only told her to have two months

off work and why at this point." She urged him on and he turned towards Sarah. "Sarah, one of our jobs..." and he indicated to Maria and himself. "...with new were-leopards is to teach them how to control themselves and not change during their most intimate moments." They watched her with a hint of concern.

She didn't know what expression was on her face, but she knew she was stunned. Sarah cleared her throat and spoke slowly so as to organise her thoughts into something coherent. "I see... And you being my chaperon will be the... the one I'll be... intimate with?" She was immensely grateful the guys weren't there.

"Yes." Antonio said cautiously.

"Okay... Logical... as it wouldn't look good for the newbies to slash their loved ones, even if it was accidental." Then she blushed and she couldn't stop it. "I haven't been with anyone since my husband's death almost four years ago." She revealed softly with embarrassment.

Out of her peripheral vision she caught them glancing at each other. Their expressions appeared to be a mix of caution and surprise.

"I'll be gentle Sarah." Antonio said tenderly as he reached across and gently gripped her hand.

Sarah blushed even harder and laughed with embarrassment. "I can't believe I'm having this conversation. I understand the necessity of it, prevention of killing one's lover and all that, but still." She gazed at Maria a little wide eyed and stunned.

'I mean... we're talking about him and I having... being...

well... intimate with each other.' She thought then said. "You're obviously okay with this."

"Antonio and I have an open and loving relationship, we're polyamorous. We became leopards at the same time, being husband and wife long before becoming therian, attacked like you were, and had to go through the same beginnings. We decided that doing this sort of education was good for the group, and it spiced up our own relationship." Maria responded with a big smile at Antonio. He gave her an answering grin and gently squeezed his wife's hand.

Sarah didn't understand the term polyamorous, but decided she would look it up on the net later when she was alone. It sounded like a whole new discussion and she just didn't need that at the moment. She took a deep steadying breath then let it out. "When do we start with the... education?" She asked still feeling rather embarrassed.

"The eating part will start with the next meal. All other aspects will start within the next day or two. As for the intimate side of the education, that will happen during the last week leading up to the full moon. The full moon is only eleven days away. It's basically a nine- to eleven-day session. The intimacy sessions will be during the three or four days before and after the full moon.

"There will be no intimacy lessons during the three days of the full moon itself. True, the night of the full moon is technically just one night. However, there are still more than the newbies who are affected by the moon on the day before and after the actual full moon."

Sarah nodded her understanding. Some of the information

being told to her she already knew, while some of it was new to her. She didn't speak, but continued listening.

"The closer to the full moon we get, the less our control is, and the stronger our emotions are, our control is that much more tenuous. Most therians avoid the personal side of things from about the fourth day before the full moon and the days just past it, just to be safe if their partner isn't therian. Also, we tend to get moody during the influence of the new moon. However, for you, we will begin with the nine-day session and go from there."

Sarah nodded, dismayed about the influence of the new moon. It was a detail she hadn't heard of during her time on the therian help line. "Over the next ten days to the coming full moon, what can I expect?" While she was still embarrassed, she was also nervous and needed the information.

"Hearing, sight, smell, speed and strength may or may not improve. You've noticed your hearing starting to improve already. How much each of them will improve depends on the individual. You may even become emotional. You might cry or become angry over something small and not know why later. It could be because of the moon or it might not..."

"So, nothing too noticeable then. I mean, I'm highly emotional in the first place so I'm not going to know if it's the moon or just me." Sarah stated plaintively with a depreciative smile.

Maria and Antonio chuckled sympathetically as Maria patted her hand. Then Antonio continued.

"First off let me state that the rest of your injuries from the attack of two nights ago won't completely heal until your first change. Yes, they are healing faster than if you were unaltered, but no they will not be completely healed before the coming full moon. The disease hasn't got a complete hold of you yet. That happens with your first change." He paused, letting it sink in before continuing.

"Injuries received from now on will heal back to their original state. As to how fast they heal will, again, depend on the individual and on your inner power. The weaker you are, the longer it takes to heal. That's part of the *something* that Jonathon mentioned earlier."

"I noticed when he spoke about it you looked like you disagreed with something he had said."

"You're more observant than I thought you were..." Antonio said his surprise obvious.

"Only because I glanced at you when I saw your expression." She explained with a slight shrug.

"I didn't like the way he made a snap judgement about you. One: regardless of whether he's right or not, he doesn't know you that well, and two: you're a jaguar, not a leopard, so the strict hierarchy won't fully apply to you. You'll be just a single voice in the league, but then there are a lot of single voices if you know what I mean. I just didn't like that Jonathon treated you like a leopard and therefore told you your place in the lepe."

"Lepe?"

"Lepe is the collective name for leopards." Maria answered.

"Ah, I see. Because they're a solitary animal, I didn't think they would have had a collective name."

"Yes, it was a surprise to us as well but it does serve a purpose now after all." Maria commented with a gentle smile.

"What about injuries received before the attack?"

"Any scars or damage received before becoming a therian will remain with you for the rest of your life. So if your arm was amputated before becoming a therian then it will still be missing after you become a therian. The therianthropy disease only recognises the current condition the body is in at the time the disease enters the system and so returns the body to that state after the change. Sorry, Sarah." Antonio informed with a sympathetic smile.

She chuckled, "Damn, I had been hoping. Was I that transparent as to why I asked?"

They both smiled as Antonio responded. "Only to those who know you Luv. Mind you, you are moving better now than you did three to four months ago."

"Yeah, I've noticed that as well, thanks to the weight loss and having regained some strength from the exercises. Will existing injuries become worse over time now that I'm therian?"

"No. The way they are at the time of one's attack will be their permanent condition. So, from this point on your ankles will not improve and nor will they worsen."

"At least that's something then, even if they were never going to get better than what they are now. What about weight loss/gain?"

"Ah I see and exactly. Well, you won't really gain any more from now on, because our metabolisms run at a faster rate from this point on. However, you will lose it to dangerous proportions if you don't look after yourself. The reason we're chaperons to the newbies right from the beginning is so we can teach them good eating habits and teach them to cook if need be. You must eat regularly and properly.

"Not only to keep from becoming underweight, but to prevent us losing control of our beasts just because we're hungry. Our beasts can break free if we don't eat properly and regularly. Unfortunately, if we don't want to be a danger to those around us, we have to look after ourselves properly. We're rather high maintenance" Antonio finished with a chuckle.

She nodded. 'So much to take in, to learn.' Sarah refocused on them when Maria took her hand in hers.

"Don't be afraid, Dear. We'll help you through this." She said soothingly.

Again, Sarah just nodded feeling a little overwhelmed.

Maria stood up then, "Go turn up the stereo and relax or do something else. We've given you a lot of information in a very short space of time and you need some time to process it all. I can find my way around the kitchen without you showing me so I'll call you when lunch is ready. Now shoo."

"Thanks guys." And she did what Maria suggested.

Allowing herself to be lost in the music, Sarah was in the sitting room unpacking her stuff the guys *he'd* organised had placed in there. 'Had to have been military guys he'd gotten to pack my stuff, because everything's flawlessly labelled in perfect, clear printing as well as being perfectly packed.' She thought as she started the task.

Her bookcases were already in place around the walls and found more bookcases had been added to the room so she could expand her book collection. The bookcases were not matching. Glancing at one of the new ones, she noted a slip of paper on one of the shelves. Picking it up, she saw it was a delivery slip with the store's name on it. Sarah decided, as money allowed, she would put her three into the other bedrooms whenever she bought a new one to match the new shelves Kaelan had bought. Once the plan was in place, she decided to start with the books first.

The first box she pulled towards her just so happened to be the books Danny had left her. Tears welled up and she had to sit there for a few minutes to try to calm herself down. However, they didn't go away; they hovered on the edge ready to swamp her if she wasn't careful. So, she sorted and shelved them, along with the rest of her books. All the while softly singing to the music coming from the lounge room; in the effort to occupy her mind on anything but her losses. Right then, the group Jethro Tull was playing; '*Aqualung*' to be exact.

...Drying in the cold sun,

Watching as the frilly panties run.

Hey Aqualung

Feeling like a dead duck

Spitting out the pieces of his broken luck...

Once finished, she stood in the middle of the room and gazed around at all her books. 'Perfect, with plenty of room to grow.'

She thought, a little happy with the way it all looked.

After the books, she slowly tackled the rest, ditching anything she didn't want any more, repacking anything that couldn't be used and set them off to one side to be given to charity.

During the unpacking she found an electronic keyboard, the musical kind. Searching the box, she tried to find a note to see who it might have been from and to whom it was for. She did find a piece of note paper, but it only had her writing on it. Skimming it, she saw it was a list of stuff that she'd been considering getting at some stage. She used to play the keyboard before the accident but had to sell it to meet ongoing expenses.

Each item on the note paper had a number beside it but they weren't in order. She had written the items out then numbered them in preference of wanting to buy or do. One of the items was 'keyboard' with a picture of one beside it, as well as a #1. However, beside that were the words 'now have', but it wasn't her handwriting.

Between Danny's books and now the keyboard she started crying quietly. The writing was *his*; he had gotten it for her. For maybe a month, give or take, the keyboard had been sitting there and she never knew. Putting it back in the box, she set it near the door.

'I'll set it up... somewhere... later, when I'm ready for it.' It took a while before she was able to stop crying enough to continue dealing with the rest of her belongings.

After lunch, which had been a quiet affair from her side of it – Toby and Mick had come back and the other four had chatted away merrily, Sarah next opened the boxes called clothing. She kept some stuff that looked good, no matter how baggy, for around the house.

'Besides, I guess they would be good to shift in. As in, it wouldn't matter if they were ruined during the process.' She thought with a shrug.

The rest of the clothing she didn't want anymore would go to charity as well. Going through them made her think about what clothing she would get next since she needed new ones; from under to outer garments. While still thinking about the possible choices, she moved onto the other boxes and decided to ditch all the little knick-knacks she'd bought just because she liked them at the time.

'There's no real memories attached to them so no use in keeping them.'

All in all, not including the books, she'd managed to cull about three quarters of her belongings. She asked Mick to chuck the stuff that was rubbish and Toby to take the rest to one of the charity places in the area. When she saw him about to grab the box with the keyboard...

"No. Not that one." She called out.

He shrugged then walked away with the rest.

She put the clothing in the bedroom, along with the keyboard and everything else, until she could work out what to do with it all.

By the time she had finished going through every box and item it was dinner time. She'd been smelling it for over an hour before Maria called everyone to the table. Sarah cleaned herself up then sat down to eat. It was amazing how dirty one could get when packing or unpacking. She tried to join in on the conversations but didn't do so well since she was almost thirty-six hours without sleep by that point. A very long day.

"You look beat, Luv." Antonio said once dinner had come to an end. "Why don't you go to bed? There's nothing that the rest of us can't do."

"I can't leave all this for you to do." She responded even though the thought of crawling into bed sounded real good right then. With her latest round of injuries still healing, she was exhausted.

"Yes you can." Maria piped up.

She looked at all four of them and was about to disagree again when Toby stood up, pulled her out of her chair and gently shoved her towards the bedrooms. All of them wore the same expression of not listening to her.

"Okay, okay. I'm going." She gave a tired chuckle. "Night all." She said and shuffled off to bed.

"Night Sarah." Was the chorus behind her as if they had rehearsed it.

When she entered the bedroom, she had a shower then flopped onto the bed dragging the covers over her. It wasn't until she'd settled that she could smell him on the pillows. Crying yet again, she cursed herself for forgetting to change the sheets on his bed. However, she was so tired she didn't stay awake long.

~*~

It was three and a half years ago when he first saw her hobbling in his general direction and, during that first time, had no idea how much she would affect him. Now, Kaelan didn't know what to do about her since she had become the very thing he hunted for a living and it was entirely his fault.

There was one person he could turn to. However, after making a call, he discovered it would be a little more than a month before the pair could talk. It was due to the fact that his friend wouldn't be back until then.

Within moments of having driven away, he had decided to make some calls. He already had an arrangement in place with his contacts to send daily to weekly reports of various happenings among the therians and vamps and their various factions in and around Brisbane and his home. It would have been foolish of him to ignore the politics of the unnaturals just because he himself doesn't like them.

Even though thinking about her hurt because of his neglect, he called his contacts to keep an eye on her and report back to him. Those he couldn't connect with at that point, he would do so later. He just had to make sure she didn't get into any more trouble.

'Amazing how she's managed to do so for someone so small.' He shook his head.

However, before even yet another day could pass, there was something else he had to do; preferably before the morning ended. The cover story she had offered up back in November was a good reason for why she was with him. While some of her words were not quite right, she'd certainly thought along the right track.

Five hours after driving away from the house and her, he rocked up to the Brisbane office of the Bounty Hunters Association and demanded to talk to the director; a man called Robert Smythe who was new to the position. Kaelan didn't care who was in the position, as the Director was going to hear about the bullshit of incomplete intel and the consequences as a result.

Over the past decade things had been changing as to how new bounty hunters became official. The powers in charge had been ditching the American-like ways of bounty hunting and were bringing in rules and guidelines better suited with existing Australian laws. Being part of the old school of one-on-one training; he'd joined during the last years of that particular training concept.

During the past few years they'd been setting up classes with official courses and graduation to be more in line with the police. Her cover story would be the last time he would be able to do/use such a thing. It was beside the point he hadn't done/used the practice in five years.

"Kaelan Ridgeleigh to see the director in regards to Job number #Q201701dash011." He stated sternly then turned away from the receptionist and sat down. He was beyond niceties by that point.

She blinked at him then made a phone call. "He won't be long Mr Ridgeleigh." She said pleasantly.

A few minutes later a woman came out and looked at him then let her eyes travel the length of him as her interest in him became obvious. "Mr Ridgeleigh? If you would come with me please?" She greeted with a more than warm smile.

By not responding to her smile, hers faltered and disappeared as a result. He was too angry to care. 'Even if I wasn't ropable I wouldn't be interested in her anyway. Oh, I guess she's attractive enough being blonde and blue eyed, 180cm tall and athletically slim.' He assessed. She was dressed in a black above the knee skirt and jacket with a red satin blouse; all of which showed off her C-cups and figure exceptionally well.

However, like all the others before her, she held no interest for him. He stood up and followed her. As she led him into the director's office he saw a large, auburn haired young man sitting in the director's private waiting area. Then Kaelan was ushered in and the door closed.

"Ah Kaelan. Good to finally meet you. I've heard nothing but good things about you." The director said as he smiled and held out his hand.

Kaelan was tempted to ignore it but gave it a brief shake before launching into his attack.

"Intel gathering around here is fucking crap! A potential hunter was attacked by a therian two nights ago and is now a therian herself as a result. All because some shithead didn't research well enough to find out that the woman with the rogue hunters was a bloody therian before issuing the contract on them. If I had known the therian was there I wouldn't have let the potential rookie be at the front of the property by herself while I was at the back..."

"Watch your language and what *are* you talking about?!" The director demanded, interrupting Kaelan as he frowned. He'd placed his hands on his hips going on the defensive.

"Job number #Q201701dash011! Two rogue hunters and one unknown woman except not a vampire. That's not good enough! Now a young woman has lost her humanity and has become one of the monsters; albeit a law abiding one. But that's beside the point. She trusted me. It was her first job and now she's therian. Do something about the intel gathering or it will be more than just words I'll exchange next time."

Only because Smythe was the boss, Kaelan managed to keep a civil tongue in his head second time round. He watched the director's hands fall from his hips and the colour drain at the hunter's words. Whether it was his information or his... warning Kaelan didn't know. He didn't care.

When angry he didn't yell, scream or even raise his voice. While he might swear, the opposite in fact would happen; his voice would go low, deadly quiet and *that's* when he was at his most dangerous. His men had told him so numerous times.

"I'm sorry Kaelan. I truly am. However, back off on the threats and... you do know that's not how we gain new recruits anymore don't you? She should have registered here and then attend the courses if accepted. These new rules and regulations are in place to prevent exactly this sort of thing."

Kaelan knew he was pushing the boundaries between employer and employee but he was angry; both at them and himself, and Smythe became the easy target. As for Smythe's question, he decided to lie outright. Not to cover his own arse – that he didn't care about, but just to spare her from the repercussions of taking revenge.

"No I hadn't been informed. I rarely come here and I didn't

receive an email or anything via regular mail." What he had stated was the truth regardless of the fact he had researched the new rules, but decided not to mention that detail. "I'd started training her the way I was trained. Make sure all hunters know from now on so none of this happens ever again. That and better intel gathering before assigning a mission."

Smythe frowned and sighed. "Well, now you know. I'll deal with both of those issues as soon as we're finished here…" Smythe started to say.

While he sounded sincere, Kaelan reserved his judgement and would wait and see. He started to leave.

"…before you go Kaelan… Lena, send him in please." He said after he pressed the intercom button on his phone.

Kaelan turned as the door opened and in walked the auburn haired young man from the waiting room. He stood 183cm tall and looked like a semi-serious body builder with pale green eyes and a tanned complexion. He had a slightly crooked mouth with one corner fractionally turned down while the other turned up a little, as if something perpetually amused him. The thing that grabbed Kaelan's attention about the man was his quietness when he moved.

"Kaelan Ridgeleigh this is Thaddeus Lucas. Thad is a hunter with some scout-tracking skills and has just moved here from Lockhart in far north Queensland…"

'It certainly explains the quietness of his movements despite his size.' Kaelan thought approvingly as the two men shook hands.

The director went on expounding Thaddeus's skills and abilities and, as expected, placed the two men together on a job during the end of February. Kaelan got to see Thad's capabilities first hand and was greatly impressed. He had no problems requesting the man for his team from that point on. Thad ended up saving Kaelan's life and got himself injured in the process which landed him in hospital for a month.

That became the starting point to their friendship. Thad had an incredible sense of humour and fun. Even though his humour and fun reminded Kaelan of the times she and him spent privately together, he did enjoy Thad's company.

The pair would have numerous hunts together in the years to come. Even though after a year of working together, Kaelan recommended Thad – to Smythe, to become a team leader. Not long after, Thad was given his own team with the two of them joining forces every now and then.

Their friendship became stronger every time they saved each other's lives. Kaelan was surprised over that fact because others he's known and worked with longer but *they* didn't socialise outside of the job. Not the way Thad and he would end up doing in the years to come.

As for intel... it improved, slowly, with each mission.

As a result of calling his contacts, during the coming down times between jobs, he would have plenty to read. Naturally, the ones of most interest would be the reports regarding her. Later in the same day he had left her, the first set of reports about her started arriving; much to his astonishment.

Having the leader of the were-leopards/head of the Brisbane

Therian League and the leader's second-in-command (2IC) visiting his house wasn't a surprise. Neither was seeing the leader leave. The surprise came when the 2IC stayed and, not long after, the 2IC's wife arrived with a couple of suitcases.

Kaelan wasn't sure what to think or how to feel about that last part. He decided to wait for the next report.

Chapter 3

Sarah awoke the next morning feeling a little better but her body still ached from the attack. Despite the fact she knew it would until her first change, she hoped it wouldn't interfere too much. Walking stick in hand, she hobbled into the kitchen and sat heavily in the chair to wake up some more before making herself a cuppa.

"Morning." She greeted whoever was in the kitchen since she hadn't cast her eyes towards them yet.

"Morning. How are you feeling Girl?" Mick greeted.

'Ah that's who's up.'

He walked over and placed a cuppa in front of her.

"Oh, thank you, you wonderful man. Ask me that when I'm actually awake."

Mick chuckled, followed closely by three other voices.

"Morning." She greeted them.

"Morning." Toby, Maria and Antonio greeted.

"At least you know the time of day." Antonio said followed by a hand hitting flesh.

Sarah chuckled softly. Maria had hit him for being cheeky.

"I'm sorry for shutting down yesterday and not being real social..." She started saying when Toby gently clamped a hand over her mouth.

"No apologies Sarah. You've been chucked into the deep end without a float of any kind and you aren't super-girl after all." He slowly removed his hand.

"What do you mean I'm not super-girl? I can't fly?" She stared at him in shock but thought her amused cheekiness might have been showing through just a little too much to be taken seriously. Even in her down moments, her warped sense of humour pops up every now and then.

"Oh, she's funny. Don't you think she's funny?" He asked the others with feigned seriousness. They laughed.

"Glad you are feeling better Honey." Maria said softly.

"A little." Sarah said with a small smile.

"What are we doing about your exercise programme Hon?" Toby asked.

Maria and Antonio watched them.

"I would like to keep up with it, but drop it down to a single set now as a way of just keeping fit rather than a need to lose weight." Sarah said to Toby and Mick.

The two men looked extremely relieved. Their expressions didn't go unnoticed by the two newcomers to the household.

"Good. Any particular time you want to do it?" Toby asked.

"For the time being I was thinking mornings after breakfast if that's okay."

"Sounds good. Do you still want the massage included?" Mick inquired.

"Yes please, because I'm still going to be a tad stiff. Beyond the injuries, I'm still noticing some soreness and am still tired."

"Well you would be. You've pushed yourself really hard for the last ten weeks Hon." Toby frowned with concern.

"How hard?" Antonio asked with sudden alertness.

Sarah wouldn't answer. She just stared at the table, knowing what their responses would be.

"Twelve to fourteen hours every day until she collapsed, then started all over again after two days of enforced rest." Mick dobbed her in instead.

"Shit Sarah! What were you trying to do? Kill yourself?" Antonio demanded, shock thick and obvious.

"No. I had a difficult time losing the weight so I worked harder than normal. I only lost seven kilos during those ten weeks."

"You're joking right? She's kidding right?" Maria asked her in disbelief then Toby and Mick.

"Unfortunately no, she's not." Mick answered.

"But from what you told me yesterday about the therian's metabolism, I thought dropping down to a normal daily regime would be the best thing to." Sarah stated.

"Yeah, definitely." Antonio stated adamantly with a frown.

Looking at Toby and Mick, "Oh, while I remember... What happened to my scooter?" Sarah asked.

They glanced at each other then back at her. "It was

destroyed by fire when Danny's house went up." Toby said softly.

She nodded. "Do you have the name and number of the police person in charge of the murders at all? I'll need to talk to them so I can claim insurance and get a new one."

"Uh... Yeah sure. I thought you would be really upset at having lost it like that." Toby said.

"Well, I am upset but nothing can be done about it so I have to move on. Besides, it was destroyed in a murder-arson so I can claim on it." Sarah said softly and left it at that.

After that, they had breakfast. Then Toby had her working out, upping her sets to two sets of ten repetitions instead of numerous sessions of five; now that she was only doing a single session a day. Afterwards, Mick gave her a massage then she had a shower and got dressed into fresh clothing. Sarah started to head back to the main part of the house when she stepped beside the box with the keyboard in it. She paused, staring straight ahead. 'Should I or not?'

Looking down at it, she then bit the proverbial bullet. Bending down and grabbed the box, she took it into the lounge room and sat on the coffee table with the box between her feet. Slowly, she opened it and took all the components out just as slowly.

Her previous keyboard had been a second hand old one, nothing flash. The one in front of her was new and she didn't know that much about it other than the basic playing of it. 'I'll never be a concert pianist and I can't read music that well and definitely can't write it, but I do love to play.'

So, with a soft sigh, she set it up. It came with its own stand

and a backless seat. After all pieces were put together she placed them near the stereo and walked away from it. She wasn't ready for it yet. Instead, she phoned the police so she could get the ball rolling for making an insurance claim on her scooter. Once that was done, she pondered what to do next.

In the kitchen, Sarah decided to work out what to have for dinner since she couldn't see anything taken out. She also decided to acquaint herself with what was in the kitchen and where. Having been in the house for just over three months, all she knew was where everything was to make a cup of tea and grab something from the fridge.

All appliances were the latest models and matching – brushed metal with black accents. He really did like to cook. His kitchen was a home chef's delight; it was fully stocked with anything they could want.

'Sort of a shame, in a way, that I'm not totally domesticated. I can cook but just basic stuff unfortunately.'

The only things she couldn't see were anything higher than her head. 'I'm so blasted short.'

"What are you doing?"

Sarah jumped so high in fright she hurt her ankles and had to grip the island to help ease the pain. "Maria, you scared the daylights out of me." She gasped through the pain and fright.

"Oh Sarah I'm sorry, didn't mean to frighten you. Sit. Go on." She helped the new therian to a chair at the table. "But what were you doing, Dear?"

"I was acquainting myself with the kitchen. I've been here roughly three months and I only know how to make a cuppa.

The others did all the cooking and cleaning."

"Oh Honey! Take advantage of that. Not often a man will do all that when there's a woman around." She said with a laugh and patted Sarah on the shoulder.

"Well, you and Ant won't be here forever so I'll have to know where everything is so I can start doing this stuff for myself."

"Maybe so, but if Toby and Mick offer, let them." Maria stated, exaggerating the last two words.

Sarah couldn't help but laugh at Maria's reaction. It was so animatedly Italian.

Just then the three men walked in.

"Hey Sarah. What's with the keyboard next to the stereo? I don't recall seeing it around before." Toby asked.

"I found it amongst my stuff. It seems to be a gift." She responded quietly.

"To you?" Mick asked, eyebrows rising.

"Yeah."

"You mean you can play it?" Mick asked. If his eyebrows rose any further, they would be in his hair.

"Yeah." Was all she said again. She had a nasty suspicion where the questioning was heading.

"You can play the keyboard *and* sing?" Toby asked incredulously.

"You can sing?" asked Antonio.

"Oh, don't you start." Sarah cried plaintively at him, feeling so embarrassed she could feel the heat creeping over her face.

The men just laughed at her reaction. The five of them sat

down to lunch, then after lunch they enticed her to play the keyboard. Their enticing was her nasty suspicion confirmed.

"I haven't played for years and I'm not that good." She warned them.

"I think she's making excuses." Teased Mick.

"I'm inclined to agree." Antonio stated then received a whack from Maria. The rest of them laughed.

"Just play Sarah." Toby ordered with a grin.

"Well, I warned you." And she set about playing.

Sarah couldn't remember the name of the piece she was playing, but it was an instrumental. She knew she was making mistakes, but kept playing anyway. Then she did what she loved doing the best. After playing a piece, Sarah started changing it into something different. Sometimes they ended up as another existing piece of music, but other times they would sound different, unusual.

If mistakes appeared in the modified version then it wasn't as bad because a lot of the time it wasn't as obvious to most except to herself or those truly into music. After a while she noticed it was dark so called it quits and they had dinner. The others ribbed her about 'not being able to play'.

"I don't know why you never made a career out of music, Girl." Mick stated.

"I told you, I'm not that good. I make too many mistakes."

"Well, I didn't notice that many of them." Antonio said.

"Trust me, those who know music really well would notice. Besides, it's just a hobby for me." She finished softly with a shrug.

"Just like your singing?" Toby asked.

"Yeah. I just get too shy... embarrassed when I do them with an audience."

Toby and Mick laughed. "Oh ain't that the truth." Mick said.

Then he and Toby delightfully regaled Maria and Antonio about the first time they had heard her sing. Then all four were laughing. Sarah just gave a small smile and blushed profusely. Then, because the stereo was on, they encouraged her to sing.

They wouldn't let up until she did. By the time she gave in, she heard Kylie Minogue's 'Can't Get You out of My Head', so sang that for them. It wasn't until she had started singing it that she realised it was the wrong one to sing at that point in time, but continued to sing it. However, Sarah refused to sing more after that; pleading tiredness.

By the time they had finished dinner and Sarah sang that one song, she was tired. Saying goodnight to everyone, she went to bed. She cursed herself for forgetting to change the sheets yet again.

Chapter 4

Sarah crawled out of bed, had breakfast, worked out, had a massage, a shower then sat at the table enjoying a second cup of tea while staring outside. The day outside was rather reasonable and promised to be a hot day. She just hoped there would be a breeze as she wasn't a fan of summer at the best of times. Eventually Maria and Antonio sat down with her.

"You might want to get changed as we'll be socialising today, Luv." He said.

"Sorry, but this is the best I have. I haven't had a chance to shop for new clothing since losing weight." Sarah blushed.

"Oh, Honey, don't be embarrassed. Things are moving rather quickly for you. We'll take you shopping first then we'll socialise." Maria said.

"Socialise?" Her voice squeaked a little. She was never good at socialising. The bigger the group the worse she was.

"Yes. You're therian now so you have to mingle with them. For the most part they'll treat you well enough. Soon, however, some of them will try to see how tough you are." Maria continued.

The way she felt must have shown on her face because Antonio gripped her hand. "It's okay Luv. If you want or need protection just come to us and ask one of us and we'll protect you." Antonio soothed.

However Sarah didn't feel soothed. She was nervous as hell.

So the three of them went shopping and bought about five full outfits that could be mixed and matched... Pants and tops because Sarah wasn't that comfortable in skirts or dresses unless they were at least ankle length. Unfortunately, she couldn't find any she liked at the time. Changing into one of the outfits in the ladies room at the shopping centre, they then 'socialised' which consisted of Maria and Antonio reintroducing her to people she knew, but as a fellow therian this time.

It was only because she knew them from before Danny's death that Sarah was able to remember them. It would be when she started meeting those she hadn't met that she would have problems with. Even though she knew the people she had socialised with that day, it was still difficult for her.

She was shy and the meet-and-greet was full of "welcome to the family" and "so sorry to hear about the attack but you're still alive" speeches. Sarah was glad when they had left because it meant she didn't have to try to be nice any more. 'I can do it in small doses but not hours on end.' She thought tiredly.

When they got home she sat on the lounge to rest, only to fall asleep. She was that tired.

When Sarah awoke the next morning she was in her bed. She just shook her head at her own patheticness...

'is patheticness a word? Oh well, it is now for the moment at least.'

...and got dressed for the workout. She hoped she would get over the tiredness soon now her exercises were greatly reduced.

She had just finished making herself a cuppa as the others entered the kitchen. They chorused "good morning" to each other.

Maria made breakfast and all ate as they discussed what would be happening for the day. After the workout and shower, the three of them would 'socialise' some more, then in the afternoon Maria and Antonio would teach her some cooking. And so their day started.

The second round of socialising was as bad as she had feared. Spread out over four different venues, Sarah spent most of her time quiet. She mostly smiled but did speak when spoken to. She was just tired of the same little speeches and greetings she had received the previous day. The last meet-and-greet included lunch to which she was grateful for as it gave her the excuse for being quiet. Difficult to talk with mouthfuls of food was her private thought.

'But really, I am rather hungry.'

When Maria and Antonio said they were heading home, she was immensely grateful but kept that fact to herself behind a small pleasant smile.

After the three of them got back home, but before the cooking lessons, Sarah entered the master bedroom and decided she had to sort out where she was going to store her clothing. The wardrobe and tallboy still had his clothing in them so she had to work out something for both of their clothing because she didn't want to live out of boxes.

Even though she wasn't expecting to see him ever again, she couldn't bring herself to pack his clothing into boxes or the spare room. Starting by removing everything from the wardrobe and tallboy onto the bed, she discovered she didn't have to sort anything out because he had already done so.

Everything was so neat, yet it didn't surprise her. The only thing she did do was remove them all quickly so she wouldn't dwell on him. It was difficult though because she was suddenly surrounded by the smell of him once she touched his clothing. Regardless, tears fell even though she tried to stop them.

Once having placed her clothing in the four top drawers of the tallboy, she started replacing some of his. However, she did have trouble with placing his clothing in the two lower drawers due to her ankles. After that, she tackled the free-standing wardrobe and was thankful it was rather large compared to the standard wardrobes.

It allowed her to place his stuff back in on the left hand side. Due to squashing his stuff together, it took a third of the space. However, that third was the equivalent of half the space of a standard sized free-standing wardrobe. Sarah decided to claim the other two thirds of the wardrobe, even though her stuff didn't even take up a quarter of the remaining space at that point in time. While she knew she would eventually have more than him, she knew she would have less than most other women.

'Even though I like pretty clothing, I'm not a slave to fashion.' She mused as she gazed at the available space.

Once that was done, she then began placing the rest of his clothing from the tallboy onto the top shelf in the wardrobe. It was the logical place for them since she couldn't reach it properly. As it was, she had to use a step ladder to place his clothing up there.

It was at that point she decided she needed to go shopping for herself. Not just for clothing – which she was in dire need of – but toiletries and perfume. Sarah was a lover of a particular brand of rose perfume and knew they had a nice range of scented products to meet her needs. So she thought it was time to get back into treating herself with their range.

After remembering Toby mentioning to Mick about discovering more bedroom furniture stored in the garage, she went down there. Rummaging around a bit, she found a dressing table with a matching high backed chair she thought was beautiful. Even though it wasn't ornate, it appeared to have been stripped back and lightly stained and varnished in a satin finish. The frame of the chair had been finished to match the dressing table – which matched the wardrobe, while the fabric matched the coloration of the room with its gold threaded ivory and pale creamy yellow brocade fabric.

After unwrapping the thick storage plastic off them, she enlisted Toby and Mick's help. They carried the table up into the bedroom while Sarah carried the chair one handed. It was slow going but it gave the men time to place the table in the room without her being under foot. When she got there it was in the best, and only, place it could be. After getting them to adjust the position of it, she then set about cleaning it down. Afterwards, she then placed what personal items she had inside.

Next, she cleared out the bedside tables to sort them out then shoved everything specifically his back into the one beside the french doors. Sarah decided to claim the side closest to the main door and the en suite. Especially the en suite due to her ankles. Everything else, she left the way he'd had it.

Lastly, she moved onto the en suite. After packing whatever toiletries he had left behind to one side of the bathroom cupboard, she placed her meagre...

'Yes! Small amount honestly.' She mused to herself.

...supply of toiletries in their designated spots. Once done, she went back into the bedroom and collapsed on the bed, staring up at the ceiling. His scent wafted around her. 'Blast! This is going to be difficult. I just hope it won't be too bad for too long.'

With a sigh she finally changed the bed covers.

By late afternoon she was in the kitchen being shown simple, but fulfilling, recipes that would help keep the beast under control. Maria handed her three lovely home-bound, computer printed books that were full of easy recipes. Sarah flicked through the pages.

Maria had printed them out on a mock parchment-looking paper with step-by-step colour photos and instructions for each meal. All of them nicely decorated in the same theme so they appeared to be a set. One book was for breakfast and lunch, the second book was main meals of all kinds and the third was soups, snacks and desserts.

Once Sarah had received the second book, she started looking for the chicken and fish based meals as they were her favourites. Sure, she didn't mind beef, lamb and pork, but chicken then fish were the ones she tended to choose first. However, she was happy to skip them if leg of lamb roast was on the menu.

'Especially if a nice thick mint sauce is available.' She mused to herself.

That night they were having a chicken risotto; Maria was cooking it to show how it was done. While watching her, Sarah organised a basic garden salad to have on the side if anyone was interested. After dinner they encouraged her to sing and play the keyboard again; until she was too tired to continue.

Minus the re-organisation of rooms, the past couple of days became their daily routine.

Chapter 5

Sarah awoke with a start. Then, for some reason, her mind furiously started working out what day it was. When it told her the answer, she groaned. The coming evening was to be the first night of the lessons to control issues during... intimacy. Suffice to say she was nervous and wasn't looking forward to it.

'Oh sure, Antonio's an attractive man, but he's married despite what the pair of them say. Then, there's the other issue... Kaelan. I sort of feel like I'm cheating on him, and we aren't even a couple. Hell! There's a chance I'll never see him again but I still feel as if I'm cheating on him.'

Staring at the ceiling she sighed, then hauled herself out of bed, got dressed and left the room to start the day. She couldn't hide no matter how much she wanted to.

After breakfast, she sent Toby and Mick downstairs to wait for her so she could talk to Maria and Antonio alone. "Ummm... I don't mean to be a pain or difficult." She paused and they waited for her to continue. "The... lessons we're to have tonight. I can't do them in this house... his house." She finally blurted out, feeling her face grow rather hot.

"Oh Luv, is that all? We can go elsewhere if you like." Antonio said.

"Please. I don't know where, but just not here. I'm sorry." Sarah felt so silly in regards to the whole situation.

"Don't apologise, Honey. It's not easy to do this in another man's home. We have backup places just for situations like this." Maria told her gently.

With relief temporarily sweeping through her, Sarah nodded, paused then went downstairs to begin her exercises. They were only semi successful in distracting her. For the rest of the day, until Antonio and Sarah had to leave, she read. She buried her nose in a book that she had read numerous times but still loved immensely. It was the only way to keep her mind occupied.

When she saw him again later that day, Antonio was wearing a made-to-order grey suit. Sarah had to admit that he looked stunning. She had never seen him dressed up like that before. He was clean shaven and smelled spicy and fresh and she was surprised to discover that she liked his scent. That she had since first meeting him. That, too, surprised her. Until that moment, she had never given such matters much thought.

However, she was now embarrassed because she knew she wouldn't look as good. While Sarah had managed to go shopping for more clothing, she knew she didn't have anything for going out. After seeing him come out, she just stared at him. The sight of him distracted her from how much she liked his scent.

"Go and get dressed Luv. We'll leave shortly." He smiled as he walked passed her; seemingly oblivious to her embarrassment.

Sarah opened her mouth as he passed only to close it again. Thinking furiously, she made her way into the bedroom and stared helplessly at the contents on her side of the wardrobe. While the clothing was new, none of them were designed for going out that matched Antonio's style. The outfit Kaelan had bought her for the hit would have been acceptable. Only, it had been destroyed during the attack and the matching shoulder bag had disappeared that same night. Then there was a knock on her bedroom door.

"Yes?"

Both Antonio and Maria walked in. Sarah wanted to say something but couldn't get the words, any words, out. One look at her and they smiled.

"Relax Dear. We have something for you." Maria said gently.

From behind his back he revealed, with a flourish, an ankle length black satin a-line dress with a deep forest green lace overlay. The skirt of the lace flared more than the under-dress. There were no sleeves and the neckline of both was a plunging V. She slowly took hold of the dress, gazing at it then looked up at them.

"It's gorgeous, thank you. You didn't have to..."

"Shhh. We know and we also knew you didn't have anything like this. We'll see you when you come out." With that, they left her staring after them with her mouth hanging open.

Giving herself a little shake, she showered, dressed, did her hair and applied a little make-up. Rummaging in a little trinket box, she found an enormous pair of clip-on fake emerald earrings and attached them to her black slip-on shoes to dress them up a little. Having only a simple black bag, she had no choice but to use it.

'Must add evening purse to my personal shopping list.'

Looking in the mirror, she noted the V of the neckline plunged to the lowest part of the valley between her breasts. The fabric covered the majority of her tattoo; except the tips of the wings and where the tail feathers trailed from one breast to under the other. Scrutinising that area closer, she noted that her weight-loss included losing the bulk of her already small breasts.

She sighed sadly. Then, taking a breath, she walked out.

Butterflies fluttered franticly inside her, she was so nervous. Not just for the way she looked but also for the time ticking closer. Her shyness kicking in, she was looking at the floor as she entered the kitchen. Maria came up to her and hugged her.

"You look beautiful Honey." She murmured.

"Come on Gorgeous, it's time to go." He smiled and the look in his eyes was one of desire and Sarah blushed.

She followed him. At 6:30pm they left the house and the drive was silent as she was too nervous to say anything.

Antonio took Sarah out to dinner to a lovely little Italian restaurant in Teneriffe she had never heard of before. It was intimate with décor in cream, royal blue and white. There were low-growing palms and low lighting and he basically wined and dined her.

"You really are beautiful Sarah."

She blushed then murmured so softly he wouldn't have heard her if he hadn't been therian. "You don't need to say that."

He reached across the table and took her hand, lacing his fingers with hers. "I may not need to say it Luv, but you need to hear those words. Ever since I first met you, I've noticed how alone you've been, how shy you are. I know you don't love me..."

Sarah held her breath dreading what he would say next in that low intimate voice meant only for her. Hoping he wouldn't say what she thought he would.

"...but that's okay because nor do I love you in that way..."

Relief flooded through her because she didn't want to hurt him.

"...however, since getting to know you I have wanted to show you how attractive you are. As much as I hate the fact that you're a victim of an attack, I won't hate this moment. I'm glad it's me who was chosen as your mentor, that you chose to call me in your moment of need. You're fragile and because of that, I will never lie to you. I adore you very much. I do think you are very pretty and tonight, you are beautiful."

Sarah blushed harder and whispered. "Thank you Antonio." She had never thought of herself as fragile and couldn't form the words to ask why he thought she was. Therefore, the moment to ask had passed.

He smiled. "Let's order."

'One day, if I remember, I'll ask him why he thinks of me that way.'

The menu was in Italian and she blinked at it in confusion.

Antonio chuckled. "While there is an English version, they know Maria and I. Do you trust me?"

With trepidation and gently biting her bottom lip with a small nervous smile, she slowly nodded.

Once the waiter arrived, Antonio started ordering. She just watched him as he spoke rapidly to the waiter in Italian. Then, with a smile, the waiter walked away and the pair lapsed into silence. A few minutes later, the waiter arrived with a bottle of wine and a bottle of water. Antonio nodded to the waiter and the waiter poured a small portion of wine into her glass then the two men just looked at her.

It took a moment to realise she was expected to taste it to see if she liked it. So, she tasted it. It was fruity with a hint of sweetness. With a shy smile she nodded as she placed her glass back on the table and the waiter filled both their glasses then poured water into another pair of glasses for them.

They both murmured thank you. With another smile, he nodded and left.

After taking a few sips of her wine, Sarah took a breath and said softly, "I know I haven't said it yet but I think you look wonderful yourself tonight." She blushed.

"Thank you Sarah." He smiled as her comment surprised him.

Despite her nervousness, she ploughed on. "I've always thought you're attractive but I've never seen you dressed this way and you just look amazing." She blushed harder, knowing she was starting to babble. "Sorry. This just feels strange though. I feel like I'm cheating on him and, strangely on Maria as well despite her knowing about this. I know she's okay with it but... it's just the way I feel. I'm sorry." Her voice dwindled to a whisper.

Antonio gently grabbed her hand again. "Don't be sorry Luv. You aren't the first to feel that way during this time and you won't the last."

Their starters arrived. There were actually three separate dishes laid between them. Sarah didn't know the name of them but one looked like it might have been a pumpkin soup and the other appeared to be Minestrone. The other two plates were slices of plain crusty bread and another with smaller slices of crusty bread but topped with tomatoe and mozzarella. Both had been drizzled with olive oil.

They shared their soup with each other and Sarah relaxed somewhat as they ate. The plain crusty bread was to have with the soup, while the other was a starter to share. She swapped between water and wine throughout the meal. She didn't want to become drunk. Although, she thought it might help ease the situation. Except, she tended to fall asleep when drinking too much. She noted Antonio drank only the wine. She didn't know what she would do later that evening if he became too drunk.

Both made appreciative noises as they ate. A few minutes after they had finished, their waiter arrived to take their empty plates away. Sarah decided to be brave and break the silence between them.

"In all the time I've known you, I've never thought to ask you what you do for a living. Do you do anything?"

He grinned. "Not a problem Luv. I'm a landscaper. I design gardens for small and large properties, private and business."

"Really? Do you enjoy it? Are you hands-on or just the designer?"

Just then, their main meal arrived, with more crusty bread

and a dish of butter curls. Even though both had salad on the side, the mains for each were different.

His looked like chunks of salmon with spaghetti with a creamy white sauce of some sort, while hers seemed to be a fried looking ravioli of some sort with a tomatoe based sauce. When she bit into one, she was surprised to discover the pasta tasted like potatoe. It was filled with a bolognaise style minced meat and tasted wonderful.

Again, they shared and resumed their conversation between mouthfuls.

"Yes I am and am both. I do love it. I love the smell of freshly dug earth and the plants and I love seeing the clients expressions when they see their dream or vision completed." Then he eats a mouthful of his dinner. "But what about you? This is the worst I've ever seen your nails. Do you enjoy being a nail tech?"

"How did..."

He laughed. "I could smell the chemicals on you. The acrylic is a powerful smell and permeates everything on you when you work with it."

She smiled. "Yes it does and yes I do enjoy doing nails. For the past three months I had concentrated on getting better, then losing weight that I didn't have time to do my own nails..."

"You do your own?" He sounded so surprised.

"Yes, I do my own nails. I'm rather fussy about the way I want them to look..."

"Well, they looked marvellous Luv."

She blushed lightly at the praise. "Thank you. Lately, all I've had time to do is file them short. After the full moon maybe I'll be able to start doing them again."

Once finished, their plates were taken away.

"You should Luv, and in a month to two months' time we'll see how you're progressing to see if you can start your business up again."

"I'm looking forward to it actually. For the past three or so months I haven't done anything and I feel so guilty over it."

Antonio went serious. "Don't Luv. In such a small space of time so much has been thrown at you, health wise. I'm surprised you've managed to survive at all. To get where you are now, you've had to concentrate on you. For that, there is nothing to feel guilty about."

Before Sarah could say anything, their desserts arrived. Gelato. That one she knew. Having a taste, she discovered hers was chocolate and hazelnut. She loved it. Trying his, it was raspberry and was surprised to discover she actually liked it as well. Once finished...

"Would you like a tea or something Luv?"

She sat back and placed a hand on her stomach. "Uhhh... no thanks. I think I'll burst if I have anything more."

His smile was wide in amusement. "Then we'll relax for a bit before leaving. Did you enjoy dinner?" He asked softly.

"I did thank you Antonio."

"My pleasure Luv. One of the beauties of having a faster metabolism is that we can eat like we did tonight and not suffer the weight issues."

"What about our hearts? Wouldn't this much food harm us

that way?"

"As long as the food's reasonably healthy, no it won't. However, our metabolism and our changes will be our eventual enemies." He was glad they both had better hearing so they were able to keep their conversation so private in the crowded room.

"I don't understand." She frowned with confusion.

"While we heal well and fast, both the changing from human to beast and back, and the metabolism puts a strain on the heart the healing can't keep up with. The heart is a muscle that is always working regardless of what we're doing. Let me put it this way... the cpu of a computer will only last so long regardless of the fan, heat sink and updates applied to it. Eventually, regardless of the updated technologies, it will be too strained to keep working.

"The more we change the shorter our lifespan. It's the one thing the stories don't have right about us."

"I see. I must admit I'm glad I'm not going to live forever. I don't think I could handle that."

Antonio nodded with an understanding smile. In silent agreement, they paid the bill and left. Driving slowly, he took her to an apartment owned by the lepe and arrived a little after 9:30. The apartment was nothing special. It was modern in an off white with muted greys and browns throughout. The occasional splashes of colour were paintings, cushions and a rug.

"Would you like anything Luv?" He was closer to the kitchen while she was next to the lounge and near the door.

She shook her head then her eyes widened as he slowly walked towards her. She couldn't help noticing he didn't appear to be drunk at all. Not even a little bit. Her heart started racing. "I-I can't Ant..." She whispered.

His expression became sympathetic as he neared. "I'm sorry Luv." He said quietly then gently wrapped his arms around her. "We must do this. I know it's been so long and that you do love another, but I promise I'll be gentle."

He tilted her head and wiped at her tears. Then, softly he kissed her, lifted her into his arms and carried her into the bedroom. After setting her on her feet he took off his jacket, folded it and placed it over the back of one of the two chairs in the room. Then he slipped off his shoes and socks. Once standing in front of her again, he cupped her face and kissed her again but with more passion that time.

"Undo my shirt Sarah and run your hands over my chest." He murmured. With only light from outside shining in, it made the situation seem intimate and romantic.

With her heart pounding hard and fast in nervousness, she had never heard his voice so low and husky like that before. The sensual-ness of it sent tingles through her. Despite knowing she had to go through with that side of the training, she cursed herself for being so weak in not pushing him away and running for her life. Instead, she did as he instructed.

One by one from the top, she undid the buttons and was surprised to see the light to medium sprinkling of dark hair. They formed the shape of a T as they went from nipple to nipple then down the centre of his chest to disappear beneath the waistband of his pants. Placing her hands on his stomach, she slowly caressed upwards sliding his shirt out of the way.

He had muscles and that also surprised her since his clothing, what she had seen him in for the past year at least, hadn't shown them off. Her fingers danced lightly across his abs and into the shallow valleys that separated them. For the most part, she tried to think of nothing but she couldn't help liking the feel of his flesh beneath her fingers. But what did surprise her was how turned on she was beginning to feel.

While the hair on his chest wasn't soft, they weren't coarse either as her fingers slid through them. His muscles clenched as he held his breath at her soft touch. Slowly, hesitantly, she ran her hands up his chest; her eyes locked on the flesh beneath her fingers. Upon reaching his upper chest, her fingers fanned out as her hands parted ways caressing their way to a nipple each.

Again he reacted in the same way as the palms of her hands skimmed lightly across them. Lowering her hands slightly, she let her fingers play with his nipples and the hairs surrounding them. Then she slid her hands under his shirt and gently pushed it off his shoulders and down his arms until it had fallen to the floor. Her fingers followed the shirt down his arms to fall to her sides when the shirt landed on the floor.

"Now my pants Sarah." He whispered huskily. He hadn't, and still wasn't, touching her since he had set her on her feet.

Her breath caught in her throat. Even without the huskiness in his voice or touching him or looking at him, she knew he was hard and aroused. With shaking hands, she reached for his belt. Her fingers fumbled a little as she undid the belt then the button on his pants. Starting to remove her hands, her mouth opened to say she couldn't do it when his hand cupped her cheek and lifted her face to his.

"Slow and gentle Sarah. We have the time." He murmured.

With their eyes locked, she lowered the zipper and his pants slid to the floor. He stepped out of them and she was surprised to discover he was wearing underwear. Wide eyed and breathless, she just stared up at him.

"Touch me Sarah."

With an exhale she didn't think she could make, she closed her eyes and tentatively touched his erection. Her fingers skimmed lightly over the fabric covered hardness and found the head by touch alone. Antonio groaned and she could sense his need. Her fingertips feathered softly along the rim of the flare to the head of his penis and his body shuddered slightly.

Then he pulled her tight against him and whispered with a harshness borne of desire and need. "My turn or I'll explode if you keep doing that."

While still very nervous, his words pleased her since she knew she was fumbling through the caressing.

From behind her back, his hands slid slowly down to the small of her back then across her waist until they reached her stomach. Being ticklish, she shivered in response, but privately she admitted to herself that his touch felt rather nice. He smiled at her reaction.

With his thumbs caressing her through the fabric of her dress, he slid his hand up over her ribs until he reached her breasts. Then he did to her what she had done to him and more. His caresses caused her nipples to harden and he bent down to suck them through the material.

She had read where women found the sensation orgasmic and wondered if she wasn't normal when she didn't. She did enjoy what he was doing to her but it wasn't orgasmic. She didn't know what to do with her hands so she placed them on his shoulders and, every now and then, her fingers would move slightly in a hesitant caress. To her, they seemed more like they were twitching.

As he straightened, she dropped her hands from his shoulders. When their eyes met, his expression told her it was the point of no return. However, the moment she had touched his erection she knew then there would be no stopping what was yet to happen.

He slid his fingers under the straps of her dress and started to lift them from her shoulders. Even though it was inevitable, she reluctantly raised her arms and Antonio slowly pulled the dress over her head. Sarah started feeling self-conscious about her body. While it looked reasonable for having lost the weight, she didn't like that fact she had lost so much from her breasts. She was just glad they didn't sag like some tended to do.

He stared at her. She didn't know if he was disappointed with her breast size or shocked at discovering her tattoo. She went to step away from him as tears welled in her eyes. Before she could complete the move, he swept her into his arms and held her firmly against him. The hair on his chest tickled her bare breasts.

"I don't say this to any other than my wife in this moment but... God, you're beautiful!"

Sarah couldn't respond and just buried her face against his chest as the tears fell.

Then he scooped her into his arms and laid her gently on the bed, removed his jocks and stood there for a moment or two just gazing at her. The moment he stood, she understood why he wore jocks. His erection pointed straight out. The underwear was to prevent obvious tenting of his pants.

Laying himself beside her, he played with her tattoo as he caressed her breasts then started suckling them in earnest. She had thought her husband had been a rare man with the attention he had lavished on her during their love-making. However, there was Antonio paying the same attention to giving her pleasure. Again, while she enjoyed the touches, she didn't find them orgasmic; just pleasurable.

Gradually, he started moving lower and her heart rate sped up a little. She knew he had to have noticed it but he ignored it as he feathered kisses and little nips as he inched his way down. Once between her thighs, he kissed her as if he was kissing her mouth. Despite thinking she couldn't go through with it, she realised she was wet; and that was before he had made his way down her body.

Then, with flicks of his tongue and nips with his teeth he attacked her clitoris and pussy with such attention that had her hips bucking in pleasure. Her instinct was to place her hands in his hair and hold on. Instead, she scrunched her fingers in the sheets as she rode the roller coaster of pressure of her building orgasm as it rose and fell as he eased or pressed forward his attack.

When he started sucking her clitoris, his fingers probed deep inside her and found that sensitive spot and she knew she was lost. She wasn't vocal in her pleasure. She did gasp and pant, but it was her writing that emphasised her arousal. His hands held her tighter as her hips bucked, sometimes away from him and other times closer to him. Then, as her orgasm hit she felt like she was going to shatter.

Without giving her a chance to recover, he settled his hips between her thighs and the head of his erection pressed at her entrance. Once again, she was full of apprehension as she stared up at him. With his hands gripping her hips, he held them off the bed as he knelt over her. Bending down to her, he kissed her – she could taste herself on his lips and tongue – and slowly pushed his way inside her.

With a groan of pleasure, he entered her gradually until he was completely inside her. At first, it hurt a little like she was a virgin once more. She felt the stretching and was afraid she would tear. Once he was all the way in, he paused and leant his forehead against hers.

"God, you're so tight." He murmured, his breathing long and deep as if he was trying to keep control of himself.

Then he started to move, sliding out slowly only to push himself back in. And so he made love to her. It was the only way to describe his actions and she became lost in the feelings, the passion, the pleasure. Because she was still feeling the effects of her earlier orgasm, it wasn't long before the second one hit.

Like waves on the beach, her orgasm rolled through her over and over. Her legs pressed tight against his buttocks as he continued to thrust himself into her. She cried out but it was barely above a whisper; more like a noisy exhale. Again, she felt like she was going to explode as she dug her fingers into the sheets.

Just when it was becoming too much for her, he came. He buried himself deep inside her and held her tight as he pumped his seed; spasms running through him with his release. Her muscles clenched around his shaft, holding him tight inside her. They stayed that way until their breathing started to settle. Spent, they both collapsed to the bed; he landed beside her, half on and half off her.

Then, much to his chagrin, she burst into tears.

"Sarah?! What's wrong?"

She covered her face as she tried, but failed, to stop crying.

"Did I hurt you?" He sounded so upset that he might have.

Still unable to control herself enough to speak, she just shook her head in the effort to ease his worries. He had been the perfect gentleman and had been so gentle with her. He wrapped his arms around her to hold her and comfort her until she calmed down enough to tell him why she was crying.

"The emotions... the feelings... the pleasure... were all too much after so long without." She managed to whisper brokenly before more tears fell.

Relaxing with her explanation, he held her tight against him and just comforted her. Eventually, they fell asleep with him spooning her from behind.

Chapter 6

When Sarah awoke the next morning she was startled to feel a body snuggled against hers. Then she remembered why there was a body there in the first place and felt herself starting to blush.

"Mmmm... Morning Luv." Antonio whispered in her ear sleepily as he started tracing her white panther tattoo on the back of her left shoulder. He had done that with the rainbow bee eater on her right breast the night before.

Shivering at the sensations it caused. "Morning. Don't do that it tickles." She whispered.

He laughed; caressing a little firmer so it wouldn't tickle as much. "Such a surprise these beautiful tattoos. I also noticed you had piercings at one stage. Why did you remove them? You didn't have to just because you became a therian."

"I didn't. The doctors did while I was unconscious from the attack. Are you saying we can still have piercings?"

"Yes exactly. Just don't use silver as it will slowly poison you. Also, if you remove them again then you'll have to get them re-pierced; again."

"I see." She responded slowly as she thought about what he had said.

Chuckling again, he kissed her cheek then went had a shower.

With the sheet tucked tightly under her armpits, Sarah laid on her back staring at the ceiling trying hard not to think of the previous night and the guilt trip her mind wanted to dwell on; amongst other things. If her thoughts went where she didn't want them to then she forced them elsewhere. Not an easy thing when the mind was so determined but, as far as she was concerned, they would have been pointless.

Then she was annoyed with her thoughts for ruining what had actually been a pleasurable night; even if she was shy. She sighed in frustration and confusion over her reactions to the whole situation.

'Why can't I accept this for what it is?' She had no answer as she continued to stare at the ceiling.

Once Antonio came out, she went had her shower.

When she came out there were bacon, eggs, toast, glass of fruit juice and a cup of tea waiting for her. She sat down and started eating.

"You did well last night Sarah. No premature changing. However, tonight and tomorrow may be different." Antonio said gently.

She nodded then asked, "How bad will it be?"

"Not an easy question to answer Luv. Everyone is different, but, usually, newbies will change during the intimacy. It takes a while to learn to control the change, and then only if they're *strong* enough to do so. Some aren't and have to avoid intimacy during the time of the full moon."

Not liking that thought Sarah breathed deeply, let it out slowly and nodded. "H-how... how does one control it?" Her voice squeaked and came out quieter than she had intended.

"It's not easy to comprehend and nor is it easy to do but you have to relax and not fight the change, and keep your emotional state calm and not panic. You'll understand when it happens Luv. Honest."

'If what he says is true then I'm doomed.' She thought glumly.

Antonio took hold of her hand. "I know you're nervous, that this isn't easy for you. Just find something to keep you calm, to keep your mind off it and it will help you. Strong emotions just make it worse Luv. You mustn't fight it as that will also make it worse."

They ate during a few moments silence. Then...

"You made love to me last night. Why? And do you do that with all of them?" Since it was supposed to be a lesson, his method confused her.

He paused then gave a small sigh. "With some, it's just sex. With others it's a bit more than just sex. How I treat them is based around how they treat me. Yes I'm polite and a gentleman but the level of all that depends on their behaviour towards me and in general." He reached over and took hold of her hand. She stared at their hands.

"You are a different matter. Not in regards to you loving someone else, but in your mannerisms. Despite living in today's age, you are old world in your private life. You don't respond to the quick tumble from just anyone, where the man hops on, takes his pleasure then falls asleep or walks away. Whether you realise it yourself or not, you require the slow participation, the gentle hand, the soft voice of encouragement…"

"But to do these lessons, don't all women need that?"

"To varying degrees yes, but not exclusively. To put it crudely, some I can bend them over and take them from behind hard and fast and still achieve the desired results from them. If I was to do that to you, I believe it would cause you pain both physically and emotionally and that's not the right sort of intimacy we want. It's about reading people, getting to know them and, therefore, knowing how much I need to do to achieve the goal."

"I see." She responded quietly. Sarah was embarrassed that he thought she needed handling with kid gloves. It was beside the point she realised he was right. Then she was surprised to have learnt something new about herself.

"Taking the becoming a therian out of the equation for the moment… Just about everyone suffers bad things. Some of their own making due to poor choices and some not. You're no different. Now, adding therian back into the situation and others I've dealt with haven't had the same number of problems as you. Let's sum them up…"

"Must we?" She murmured in embarrassment.

"Yes Luv, you need to hear this. Your family rejected you. Yes, I'd managed to pick that up with some of our discussions over the past year. You're so shy you don't make friends easily and can count them on your fingers with maybe some to spare.

You lose your husband in an accident and became injured yourself that left you with a permanent disability. After making new friends you lose them in an attack and become injured again. Just in that list alone there's six before you even become a therian.

"Most might have one to three of those before the incident of becoming a therian. These things shape who we become. Unlike most others, you've retreated into yourself and it just gets worse for you with each event. You need care and attention to bring you out of yourself and to give you confidence, and if the way I treated you last night does that then I'll continue without regret."

Sarah blushed at his speech then murmured softly, "Thank you Ant. I don't know if I'll stop being nervous but I won't run from our lessons."

He smiled and gave her hand a gentle squeeze. "That's all I can ask Luv. Now, let's clean up and go home."

She nodded then did the dishes while Antonio did other cleaning. She discovered the washing machine was one of those all-in-one units with dryer functions built in. After they had finished they went back home until later that night when they would go back to the apartment.

That was the way the intimacy lessons went for the next two nights. Sarah was reminded that there would be no lessons on the nights of the full moon. Of which she was grateful for; not for the reminder, but for the lack of intimacy lessons.

*

However, the second lesson didn't go as well as the first, but she hadn't fully realised it until after the fact.

At the height of her orgasm, pain hit her and she could feel herself changing. It was worse than if she had been on a roller coaster. More intense and deeper than the feelings she would get in her stomach. She tried to stop it by pulling herself away from it, by tensing up in the effort to stop the internal movements. In doing so it caused a lot more pain. Because of the pain, she had forgotten everything Antonio had told her that morning. Her body felt like it was burning. Not just in any one or selected areas, but all over. Inside and out.

She had to let go of Antonio and dug her fingers into the mattress, hard, in an effort to ease/ride the pain any way possible; except for relaxing. Her back bowed off the bed, almost doubling back on itself, from the pain. She bit her bottom lip, refusing to scream out. As a result, it came out muted like a higher pitched crying moan than a scream. Tears trickled down her temples. So did blood flow as she bit deep into her bottom lip.

When it was over and the pain finally eased up she collapsed back to the bed and the tears flowed freely. She couldn't move. She didn't have the strength, the energy. Sarah managed to open her eyes and, through the tears, saw blood on Antonio's arms. She frowned slightly and tried to focus on what she was seeing. From shoulder to elbow he had deep furrows. She didn't understand how.

Not at first.

Antonio rolled on to the floor and it took a lot of effort to turn her head to keep him in sight. He was on hands and knees when she saw and heard his skin stretch and split and other things move. It was a scary thing to see and hear. It was her first time after all. She didn't remember the one from her own attack.

Then a golden orange fur with black rosettes started flowing all over.

Where there was once a man crouching was now a were-leopard. He shook himself all over then sat down on his hip with his head hanging down and looked at her by moving only his eyes. They stayed that way for a few minutes, just looking at each other. Him looking exhausted and her with tears flowing non-stop.

Most stories have were-creatures looking cute or turning into the full blown animal, but they're neither. The body is muscular and the hands and feet are long with exaggerated knuckles and wicked looking claws. While the face appears to be a brutal nightmarish version of the animal it's supposed to be. It's like it has more muscles that it should, allowing for such grimaces that only belong in horror stories. The nostrils flare more compared to either man or beast and the teeth are numerous, longer than they have a right to be and so sharp they could pierce through her arm easily.

However, she couldn't take her eyes off him. In his own way Antonio, as a were leopard, was attractive. Maybe it was because she could see the intelligence in his almost human eyes. Or maybe the compassion. Being exhausted, she couldn't work it out. Although, the sight of his therian form didn't last long. After a few minutes Antonio changed back. He sagged to his arms, which were whole now, and stayed there for a few moments before crawling over to her.

"Shit Luv, you shouldn't have fought it. It would have been less painful for you." Exhaustion and pain dripped from his voice.

"I'm so sorry." She whispered through the tears, because she couldn't manage anything more.

He managed to pull himself onto the bed. He looked at her then slowly and carefully disengaged her hands from the mattress. Or more to the point, he gently pulled them *out* of the mattress.

Her nails were broken with the odd few bleeding. He placed her hands on her stomach and pulled the covers over her. It would seem that her hands had changed into claws. She understood then how his arms had become injured.

"I'll be right back okay?"

She just blinked at him and watched him stagger out of the room into another part of the apartment. While watching him, some part of her thought he had a very attractive backside. Blushing at her own thoughts, she closed her eyes once he was out of sight. In closing her eyes, she noted various things in regards to her body. One of which, even though she hadn't felt it, he had ejaculated; and while still inside of her by the feel of it. The other was, she felt like she had been doing her fourteen hours of exercises again; extremely sore and aching.

What seemed like a short while later, she opened her eyes as he came back into the room. He was moving a little better than when he had left. She suspected she may have briefly fallen asleep. He had two large containers in his hands and one under each arm. He sat heavily on the bed setting them on the other side of her then took off the lids.

One was a first aid kit and he cleaned up her fingers. While the nails were broken, the skin was whole. They had healed.

"You may not feel like it but you need to eat. You'll feel better once you do."

With that he fed both of them cold-cut meats, cheese, bread rolls and fruit from the other containers. He even had a bottle of milk. She didn't feel like eating at first; she felt horrid. However, as she ate what he put in her mouth, she did start to feel better. Although, she could see he was feeling better faster than she was.

Eventually she was able to lift her hand at least to stop him from feeding her more food. "I'm sorry, I can't eat any more." She whispered exhaustedly.

"It's alright, Sarah. You ate a decent amount. You need sleep now. First, however, I'm going to lay you on the floor so I can flip the mattress so the rips are to the bottom."

He did what he said then remade the bed and laid her back on it. She was so exhausted that she slept on her back for the first time in years.

Sarah woke up screaming.

Pain tore through her body as it burned from the inside out. She rolled onto her side only to fall off the bed. Landing on her stomach as her chin hit the floor hard, she dug her fingers into the carpet. Looking on in horror, she watched them change into something that wasn't quite human anymore. She didn't try to stop it. Not because she had been told not to, but because she didn't have the energy to stop it.

She couldn't even think of anything calming. Not just because she forgot, but the sight of her hand caused all thought to flee as pain and horror overrode everything else. Her fingers lengthened, the skin stretching tighter and tighter. Blood started to seep then trickle from beneath her nails as they grew thicker and longer. It felt as if someone was trying to rip them out slowly in the effort of causing as much pain as possible.

Her body convulsed as it started to change. The fur hadn't started to flow yet when her hands seemed to be changing back to normal. Somewhere in the back of her mind she was grateful but didn't understand why the change was reversing itself so soon.

She felt a set of hands grab at her, rolling her onto her back but up onto something. It wasn't until she saw a face looming over her did she realised she was actually on their lap. Through blurry eyes she couldn't see who it was clearly but could see their mouth moving. Over the sound of the blood pounding so hard and fast in her ears, she couldn't hear them.

As quickly as the pain had come, it went and she was left panting in Antonio's arms.

"Sarah... Sarah!" He called urgently.

"Ant." She managed to choke out. She suspected he had been calling her name since she screamed.

"I told you not to fight it..."

"I didn't." She whispered hoarsely. "I couldn't."

Antonio cradled her in his arms gently rocking her as tears

flowed yet again. After a little while he lifted her up and laid her back on the bed. In exhaustion, she fell asleep.

Sun streamed into the bedroom, waking her up when it shone into her eyes. Sarah felt like she had been hit with a semi-trailer road train at top speed. She groaned. A moment or two later, the bedroom door opened and Antonio entered.

"Morning Luv. You're finally awake." He said, sounding rather subdued.

'How bad was it last night?' She thought to herself.

"Morning." She croaked. Her hand went to her throat. It hurt so much. Only then did she notice the cup in Antonio's hand.

"I won't ask you how you feel. I think I can work that out just by looking at you." He set it on the bedside table then sat beside her.

"Why do I feel so bad?" She winced in pain at trying to talk.

"Don't talk yet Luv. As to what happened... You suffered a second partial change during the night."

As he helped her to sit up, she groaned in pain again and memories of the previous night flooded her thoughts. Antonio handed her the cup but her hands shook when she tried to hold it, so he reclaimed it and helped her to drink.

"Why?" She asked. The drink turned out to be hot tea, heavy with both lemon and honey. Her voice sounded a little better but the throat still hurt.

"You were screaming Luv, that's why your throat hurts. We don't know why the partial changes happen. They're not common but they do occur. Usually during the beginning training it's a full shifting. We think, but aren't sure, that if the therian fights it then it comes back later. However, with not enough evidence and not happening every single time, we just don't know for sure." He informed as he helped her drink the tea. "I'm going to run a hot bath for you to help ease your muscles and soreness. So, just stay there until I'm done."

"Comedian." She croaked at him with a half-hearted smile. He chuckled as he went into the bathroom. Laying there, she listened to the tub fill with water. She must have fallen asleep during the filling process because the next thing she knew Antonio was carrying her into the bathroom.

"Just relax and your muscles will feel better sooner."

Then he placed her into the deep long tub with wonderfully hot water covered in bubble bath. Her feet didn't even reach the other end. Letting the water and bubble bath enveloped her, she laid her head against the back of the tub.

The next thing Sarah knew, there was water sloshing all over the place and she started coughing.

"Blast, Luv. If I knew you were going to go under like that I wouldn't have left you alone." Antonio sounded panicked, upset.

Blinking in confusion, she tried to stop coughing as lavender scented water streamed down her face and out of her mouth and nose. The bubbly foam tickled her face as it slowly slid down. Antonio sat behind her in the tub to keep her sitting up with her head above the water.

"I'm sorry. I must have fallen asleep." She spluttered and coughed a couple more times.

Antonio wrapped one arm around her waist and one across her chest at shoulder height and sighed. "I'm sorry too. I should have known better with the condition you're in." He nuzzled the top of her head.

"I hope this stage passes quickly. I really do not want to go through this too much longer." She whispered as she leant heavily against him. She was so exhausted and the day hadn't even really started.

'If I wasn't so tired, the two of us like this would be rather erotic.' She thought then felt unreasonably guilty.

"I know this isn't what you want to hear but it's just the beginning. However, I will tell you that it does get better as the months go by." Antonio responded quietly.

"Months." She moaned in despair. "Has anyone never survived the beginning?" While she was afraid, she was glad it didn't show in her voice.

"Not that I've heard. Don't let it make you afraid Sarah. If you do you'll end up feeling like you did last night, for the rest of your life, when you tried to fight it. Just let it happen and the pain will lessen each time. It will never 'not' hurt but it won't hurt as much as it does now."

'I guess he's able to sense my fear.'

"I'll try." She whispered. Then a thought occurred to her. "Why didn't anyone hear me screaming?"

"This place has been fitted with the highest possible sound proofing just for this reason."

"Ah, good idea."

When the water was too cool to enjoy they got out and she

realised she did feel much better. They dried, dressed then had breakfast before heading back home again. Why didn't they just stay there if they were going to be back again that evening? Sarah wanted out of the place for a little bit. She needed a change of scenery, so home they went.

Maria fussed over her when they got back. It seemed like Antonio had discussed what had happened with her. After the fussing and a cup of tea, Sarah rested in the sitting room for the day and promptly fell asleep.

*

The evening was a repeat of the last, all the way down to the partial changing and waking later with a second partial change. Only this time Sarah did her best not to fight it but it was difficult.

From the moment one understands the concept of pain, one is taught to fight it because if one can prevent it then the pain will go away. However, the reverse is true for therians. If they fight the pain of the change, the pain becomes worse. So Sarah was now battling twenty to twenty-five years' worth of ingrained behaviour. Either way, it was only one night before the full moon and she went through a partial change, and it hurt so very, very much.

The next morning Antonio decided if Sarah was going to suffer that badly each time then the hot bath would become a regular part of the 'education'.

While she was glad that they would be having a break from the lessons that night, it was the first night of the full moon. She wasn't looking forward to the change at all.

Chapter 7

When she woke up later that day, she just laid there and stared up at the ceiling. As much as she had tried not to think, her mind just rehashed the events of the previous three nights and the coming change that evening. Other than causing her stress, her thoughts were unproductive. Roughly an hour or so later, she hauled herself out of bed and had a shower.

After dressing into an old pair of cotton pants and a loose top, Sarah went out into the kitchen to make a cup of tea. She was nervous. The butterflies had awoken and were fluttering around madly.

'Still no one has given me a net to catch them with.' She thought apprehensively.

Toby and Mick didn't say a word when they saw her. She guessed her nervousness was obvious. But then, maybe there was nothing they could say because they didn't know what it would be like.

Then, something occurred to her that she hadn't realised before. 'I can't believe I've been a therian for ten days already come tonight.' She sighed. While most others had two to four weeks to get used to the fact and the training, she hadn't. Other than her improved hearing, and the partial changes over the past couple of evenings, she's had no indication of being a therian at all. She really felt no different. Her nervousness grew.

Maria and Antonio came into the kitchen dressed similarly to Sarah... Clothing they wouldn't mind ruining when they changed. Sarah still wore shoes though, even if they were just slip-ons. Her feet had become extra sensitive since the accident so when she stood on things they hurt more than they should have. Having gone from running around in bare feet all the time to needing shoes had been one of the things she hated, but she hated the pain more.

No one spoke. Occasionally, Maria and Antonio would murmur privately to each other, but that was about all that interrupted the quiet that had settled over the house. Eventually, it was time to leave.

The three of them arrived at a mansion-like home on a very large property on the north side of Brisbane. Maria informed Sarah it was Jonathon's house. The fence was high, topped with electrical and barbed wires and Sarah hazarded a guess that it went all the way round the property. There were security cameras, and they were active, as well as a security gate that one had to press a button to talk to someone before they would let anyone in. The driveway was long and circled around a fountain before heading back the way it came.

The house, which could be seen through the gate, was a three storey mansion-like home. It was huge and white and, as far as Sarah was concerned, totally without character. Very sterile looking but had become popular in Brisbane a few decades ago.

They went to the front door and were greeted by a real live butler named Malcolm. He escorted them to the back patio area of the house. There were other people there, as well as Jonathon and his wife Lucidia – also formal in her behaviour. There were a few other faces Sarah recognised, but not many.

They had barely stepped out to join everyone when some couple she didn't know, but had seen around on and off, came up to Maria and Antonio. The woman demanded with disdain...

"What's she doing here? Just because she helps out on the help lines doesn't mean she should be here as well."

People started turning their attention towards their little group.

Sarah was small but not small enough to disappear, and she really wanted to disappear right then. Instead, she stood still and stared down at her feet.

"Back off Julie, she's here with us." Antonio stated quietly.

"She's just a human, she shouldn't be here at all." The man pushed the point heatedly. The look he gave Sarah was one of sharp poisonous darts.

"Actually Ned, Sarah has recently become a jaguar and I invited her here." Came Jonathon's very formal, very stiff voice rather loudly from Sarah's left.

All chatter ceased. He had been heard, even over the noise of everyone else. Without lifting her head Sarah moved her eyes around and saw that everyone were either looking at Jonathon or her. She just stood there silently.

"Sarah was attacked by a rogue ten days ago. Since there are no other jaguars in Australia, I extended the hand of friendship

to her. She is here as my guest and you will treat her as such."
He only stated it but his stiff manner practically screamed his
statement like an order and he expected it to be followed
without argument.

'Well, gee! That's going to endear me to the rest of them.
Not!'

After that little speech, Jonathon and Lucidia greeted Maria,
Antonio and Sarah then told Maria and Sarah to mingle. He held
back Antonio to talk to him. Antonio was Jonathon's second in
command. So, Maria – with a small tolerant smile – and Sarah
'mingled'.

However, after a while, Sarah had to sit down because her
feet and ankles were hurting. She just sat there watching
everyone else. If someone came up to her, to 'mingle', she
worked hard at chatting with them. For the most part they left
her alone and that suited her fine. Although, it did leave her
feeling bored for the duration. While she knew it was her own
fault, for sitting on the side lines, it still made her feel awkward
being by herself.

It was almost 10:00pm when they all started to head to the
back of the property where there was bushland. Maria and
Antonio came back to Sarah to escort her with the rest of the
group. She was practically the last to enter among the trees.
Upon reaching the tree line, however, she could see some had
changed already.

Looking to her left, she saw a man fall to his hands and
knees. He was only in a pair of shorts so she had full view of his
change. Even though she had seen Antonio change a couple of
nights ago to heal the scratches she had caused, watching it

again still scared and horrified her. Others stayed standing during their transformation. After their change, they slowly disappeared deeper among the trees.

"Don't be scared Sarah. You will get used to it." Maria whispered to her. She didn't have to speak any louder. Sarah, and others, could hear her very well.

Sarah was still at the beginning line of the trees when pain hit her and she staggered against the nearest tree. Dropping her walking stick beside it, she hurriedly slipped off her shoes so she wouldn't ruin them. Another wave of pain dropped her to the ground. She couldn't kneel like everyone else so she ended up lying on her side.

"Relax Sarah, don't fight it." Antonio said softly, encouragingly.

"Just let it happen Dear. Lay there if you have to, but just let it happen." Maria coached.

Sarah tried to think of nothing, anything, but the waves of pain came faster, and shattered her thinking capabilities. Following the pain came the stretching and tearing of her skin and other things she really didn't want to know about. She screamed in agony. She couldn't 'not' scream. Her body jerked and convulsed with the changes as joints dislocated and bones and organs moved. Some by a small amount, some majorly so. Then fur started to come out. Slowly at first then faster and faster like water flowing by the time it was finished. It's entire process felt like thousands of fiery tiny ants crawling over her skin.

Finally, after what seemed like hours but was barely minutes, Sarah had changed. Sitting there with her arms holding her new upper body up off the ground, her head was bent low as she panted from the pain.

Something hit her on the leg and it took a bit of effort to look at what it might have been. Looking down the length of her body she saw very pale fur instead of orange and a snippet of memory of her attach flashed briefly in her mind. That and her clothing had survived and fitted a little more firmly than before. She noted that she didn't seem to have any of the rosettes she had also been expecting though. As she looked at what was moving against her leg, she saw a tail in the same coloured fur as her body.

Her eyes followed the length of it back up to where it was attached to her lower back where it met the beginning crease that separated her buttocks.

'I have a tail!' The thought seemed so silly she started to laugh and the sound of the laugh had her laughing harder. It sounded like a cat hissing but with a faint sound of voice... vocal, to it. 'But I have a tail.'

Slowly a golden furry clawed hand came into view. "Sssarrraaahh, arrrre you okay?" Antonio asked her.

It took a moment for her to realised he was talking. Rather awkwardly, she nodded and climbed to her feet with his help. She staggered slightly because she felt a little disorientated from the change and Antonio kept hold of her to steady her. Regaining her balance, she discovered that she could walk without any problems. Her ankle problems didn't exist in were-form.

A leopard the same colouring and markings as Antonio, whom could only have been Maria, held out her hand to Sarah,

"Come, follow us."

They turned and started to run deeper into the bushland, and Sarah ran after them.

It was an amazing feeling, to run, to feel so free and alive. The trees and shrubs just whisked by. As a human Sarah would have fallen so many times and injured herself, but as a jag she flowed through as if she ran through those trees hundreds of times.

After a while she could see a soft yellowish glow up ahead and started to slow down. A little closer, she could see the glow was caused by burning torches. Closer still, she could see they ringed the outer edge of a clearing and in that clearing were the leopards.

A large mostly black, with patches of lighter colour and hints of orange, leopard – when one says leopard they mean were-leopard because no therian turns into a full animal for real – came towards her.

"Welcome Sarah. This is our meeting place, our private social place. Come and join us without fear this night." Jonathon greeted formally, taking her by the hand and led her into the clearing. His voice was as growly as Antonio's.

Off to one side of the clearing was a curtained area. Off to the side of that were a bunch of tables and chairs stacked out of the way. In the rest of the clearing were all the other were-leopards and a... throne for lack of a better word.

Jonathon let go of Sarah's hand and Antonio and Maria led her to a small space where the three of them sat down, while Jonathon sat on the throne. Of course.

What followed was a bunch of therian-style entertainment. Some of it was brutal, males and females slashing the daylights out of each other, and full of deafening growls and roars. Then they would change into human form to heal then change back and continued if they could. The one who didn't surrender, won. Other parts were amazing feats of agility, stamina and strength. Sarah didn't really remember much of the entertainment as things got a bit hazy for her that evening.

After the entertainment the hunt was called. It turned out Jonathon had the bushland part of his property stocked with deer for the nights of the full moon. As they started prowling through the woods, clouds started creeping across the sky. After the leopards broke off into groups and disappeared in different directions, the group Sarah was with ranged in a wide circle to ensnare a deer or more.

The cloud cover thickened, as a ripple of excitement went through the group, to darken the woods even further. Sarah could scent deer nearby. All moved as one, slowly, cautiously, tightening the circle. Then one, two, no three sets of bleating of deer could be heard and those in front hunted them down. Once three of the deer were caught, the group split into three and those in front fed.

The human part of Sarah held back at the sight like she was watching some horror movie. The animal part hung back because it recognised it wasn't part of the lepe. Jonathon looked up from the carcass, blood over his muzzle and held his clawed paw-like hand out to her.

With that gesture others parted to let her partake of the offering. While the human half wanted nothing to do with it, the animal half was stronger and she stalked over. Sarah knelt before Jonathon, nuzzled his hand in greeting and thanks then buried her own muzzle into the still warm flesh. Jonathon, Lucidia, Antonio, Maria and two others resumed eating.

The hair of the deer tickled her muzzle. The flesh was warm, juicy and tender. The blood was thick, fresh and still warm even though she could tell it was starting to cool. It eased her parched throat from the run, watching the entertainment without refreshments and the hunt. She sunk her canines in and tore a chunk of meat off a shoulder and ate greedily.

Soon, there was nothing much left of the three carcasses.

Alone or in groups of two or more, the leopards started to disappear among the trees in all directions. Sarah was standing a distance away from the remains when a young male dark tannish orange leopard cautiously came towards her. She knew the leopard was a male due to the obvious sign of his genitalia. Embarrassed at such an observation, she stood there looking at him. He paused then took another step towards her, then paused again.

Eventually she realised he was asking to come closer. If she was human she would have blushed, instead she looked down then flicked her eyes back up at him. It wasn't deliberate. She behaved that way in human form when shy and embarrassed anyway.

He came up to her and tentatively licked her cheek.

Confused at first, she then figured it was one way of cleaning the blood from the fur, and in looking around she could see others were doing just that. But she was shy and didn't want to give him the wrong idea and paused again.

So, the jag in her sat on her human half and let him clean her as she cleaned him.

Sarah stirred, but kept her eyes closed, shivering slightly and realised she wasn't in bed. She woke up with her eyes snapping open and realised she wasn't in a building of any kind. Moving, she discovered she was naked. Now she was completely awake as the sleep clogging her mind had instantly blown away with that realisation.

Sarah moved her hand only to come in contact with a bare back. It was still dark and she couldn't see anything. Not at first anyway. Once her sight adjusted, she looked at that bare back and followed its line to a set of bare male hips. She scooted back wondering what in the hell had happened the previous night. Her movements awoke him.

He rolled only the top half – thankfully in her opinion – of himself over and looked at her. A smile spread across his lips, but then it faltered and the smile disappeared. She guessed her expression wasn't a good one.

Sarah opened her mouth to say something but nothing came out. She turned bright red. With the dawn growing brighter, she knew he would see it

His smile returned. "Hi, I'm Luke."

Luke with the surprisingly deep voice was tanned all over, but she sort of didn't think it was suntan. It was too even, but she didn't know what his nationality was. He had straight brown hair with soft brown eyes ringed by wonderful lashes that girls would kill for. Bit on the skinny side but then most therians were she had noticed. He looked to be about her age.

"Sarah." She squeaked out, groaning mentally with embarrassment.

"I know." He smiled widened. "Relax Sarah. I won't bite. Besides we didn't do anything."

Sarah was covering her nudity to the best of her ability as he said that and he chuckled.

"I know how it looks, but trust me, we didn't do anything other than clean each other's faces, necks, arms and hands. Look at your top and you'll see why you aren't wearing your clothes." He informed kindly.

She did inspect at her top and saw the brown stains of dry blood. Then she was surprised to note her clothing had come off intact.

Luke stood up, giving her a full frontal, and held his hands out to her so he could help her stand. With a flash of a memory of a well hung dark tannish orange were-leopard, she instantly gained first-hand knowledge of the size of Luke in both human and therian forms.

Blushing some more, Sarah deliberately stared up at his face and timidly held her hands out to him. Seeing how endowed he was, was more than she had wanted to see. He pulled her up so fast that she couldn't get her balance and fell against him. As his arms wrapped around her to support her, Sarah was blushing so hard that she was starting to feel dizzy.

However, she briefly noted she came up to his nose. 'Only a few inches taller than me. Funny what we notice at the weirdest times.'

Once he had made sure she had her balance he let go of her

then bent down to pick up her clothing and handed them to her.

"Thanks." She whispered as she started dressing.

"Thank you for your companionship last night. Not everyone shares with everyone else. I've been a leopard for three years now and it's still not easy around here."

Sarah didn't know what to say to that. "You're welcome. This is my first time as a jag so I wouldn't have a clue about anything really." She blushed some more and was hating it.

Luke smiled at her. "You got the hots for me or just shy and embarrassed?"

"Oh, you're nice on the eyes but I'm just shy and embarrassed." She blurted out then covered her face. 'I did not just say that. I did not just say that. Far out space cookies I so just did.'

He laughed. "Come on. Let's go up to the house." And he started walking away. He paused when he realised Sarah wasn't beside him. She was having a difficult time walking over the plant debris and uneven ground without losing her balance and was clutching at a tree in pain. "You okay Sarah?"

"Bare feet and no walking stick are making it painful to walk." She whispered through clenched teeth.

Suddenly, coming back to her in three easy strides, Luke picked her up and started carrying her towards the house.

"I left my shoes and stick at the tree line somewhere." She said softly as embarrassment ran rife through her.

Lying still in his arms, he gave her a smile but was a gentleman the entire time. However, it didn't stop her shyness and awkwardness from controlling her. His strides were long and rocked slightly from side to side. A loping gait she guessed. Within a couple of minutes of breaking free of the trees they found her walking stick and shoes. Luke put her down so she could put the shoes on and he handed her the walking stick.

"Rather ironic walking stick you have."

"It was a gift before I became a jag." She stated quietly.

"Beautiful gift." Was all he said as they walked towards the house as he slowed his pace to keep up with her.

It was fully dawn but the sun hadn't risen above the horizon yet. Not even peeking through the surrounding trees. Luke and Sarah weren't the only ones awake and walking back to the house. Nor was he the only one naked, and yet no one was treating it as something sexual.

'I suppose if one's clothes were ruined during the change then one would have to become comfortable with nudity. Both as a natural state of those around them as well as themselves. Boy, do I have a long way to go.'

"Sarah." Antonio sounded relieved when he called her name.

She waved at him and Maria. They were standing at the edge of the patio as Sarah and Luke joined them.

"Luke, good to see you." Maria greeted as Antonio gave her a hug.

"I'm okay Ant." She smiled up at him.

"You too Maria, Tony." Luke smiled at them then at Sarah. "Now that you're in capable hands I'll go find my clothes." And he left.

"Thank you Luke." Sarah called out softly.

"Anytime Sweetness." He said with a grin as he walked away.

"Sweetness?" Antonio said after Luke disappeared into the house.

"He said nothing happened." She responded hesitantly.

"Don't frown so Luv. He is a truthful guy."

"He did go out of his way to reassure me."

"Oh?" Maria enquired.

"I woke up naked and I guess I was on the verge of freaking out." Sarah blushed yet again.

"Oh, Luv. Sorry we didn't explain what to expect during the time of change." Antonio looked concerned.

"Don't be. I think I managed to work some of it out on the way back here."

"So why were you naked?" A mischievous glint appeared in Antonio's eyes and Maria gave him a thump in the arm.

Sarah smiled at their carry-ons. "Grooming as far as I can work out." And she glanced down at her top and they nodded in understanding.

"Come on ladies. Let's go home." Antonio grinned and they left.

Once they got back to home, they ate then Sarah had a shower, crawled onto the bed and fell asleep.

Chapter 8

The next two nights of the full moon were a repeat of the previous night; including waking up next to Luke. Even though he reassured her nothing had happened, she was still embarrassed.

After the full moon started to wane, Antonio and Sarah resumed their lessons for the next three nights. The first two of the three nights after the full moon had her suffering the dual partial changes again. Both sessions hurt tremendously though. While the last evening of the intimacy lessons was the same as the first night of the lessons before the full moon. She was immensely grateful for that piece of mercy.

She was, however, still embarrassed and shy about being with Antonio. She didn't think she would ever stop being so. It would make the next eleven or so months difficult for her if she couldn't get over her shyness and embarrassment.

'I am so doomed.' She thought miserably.

Amidst all the lessons and such, her life before becoming a therian intruded; bringing sad memories with it once again.

Legalities in regards to Brandi and Abel's home up at Caboolture were finally completed and it now belonged to Sarah. She still felt as though she couldn't live in it, but couldn't handle having anyone else live in it. She decided to give it a little more time before deciding what to do with the place. All she did know was that she wouldn't ever sell it.

*

The month following her first full moon was non-stop busy for her. Sarah spent her time exercising, socialising with other therians and vampires, learning to cook and learning some basic therian etiquette and rules. What to do and what not to do. When she wasn't doing any of those things, she started doing her own nails again and setting up her nail bar. In doing her nails, she decided to switch from the acrylic to gel.

For her first application since October last year, the other four watched her lightly file the tops of her nails – so the gel had something to adhere to – and place a form on each finger. Then they watched as she placed gel on the form from where it met with her natural nail. Next, she placed her hand in the uv lamp to set the gel.

After the lamp switched off, she then started building the layers to a thickness she was happy with, setting each layer in the uv lamp before applying the next. Once done, she then buffed them into her desired shape and smoothness then coated it with one last layer of gel for that final glossy look. Without any colour, lacquer or gel, it took her two and a half hours doing her own nails.

Her housemates asked questions each step of the way and she answered them patiently.

"You would make a wonderful trainer, you know." Antonio stated after the others had walked away as she started packing up her gear.

Sarah blushed. "Thank you, but I'm not good with people and I find those sorts of courses frustrating to do. I almost didn't make it as a qualified tech."

Antonio smiled and nodded understanding before Maria called him away.

She decided to update her nail bar's website with the new address and a make-over to match the look of her nail bar. That, the website make-over, cost her a little more than she had hoped once she had found a site designer she was happy with. On the site, she also stated she was now a therian – as per the law requirements, and that she would accept humans, therians and vampires as clients.

That part hadn't really changed as she had never discriminated in the first place. She also set an opening date with hours during which to call to make appointments. Then she set the nail bar's phone to divert so it went to her mobile. The day after she had set that information, Sarah started receiving calls for bookings. She still had a business and that made her very happy.

Also, she checked her various bank accounts, personal and business. A quick calculation and it worked out that in her private account she had enough to live on for the next four months. While her business account had just enough to cover ongoing expenses for the next three.

'Thankfully, I'll be back at work in another month or two. I really can't afford any more time off than that or I'll start running at a loss and it'll be horrendous work to get back in the black.'

Next, she did the ring-around to various companies to let them know the change of business address for things like power, phone and internet. Suppliers were easy as she just went to their websites and updated her billing and delivery addresses. The personal side had been taken care of within a few days of Kaelan asking if she had wanted to stay so that was one less chore for her to deal with.

Since just after becoming a therian, Sarah had dealt with the police and the insurance company about her scooter. The insurance company was strangely satisfied – as in without argument – with the claim report and granted her a payout to buy a new scooter. She didn't question their lack of argument, since she just wanted that chapter of her life closed, and bought another deep red Yamaha T-Max 500 with a matching top box.

New mobile phone, new scooter, new business location and appearance, and things were starting to look normal again. There were just a few more things she wanted to do for herself...

After Antonio's comments about piercings, she did some research on a couple of subjects and found two professionals who would willingly work on therians. Calling the first one, she made an appointment to see him the next day to discuss options and a possible appointment for the procedure. When the next day arrived...

As soon as they shook hands, she was surprised to discover he was a therian.

"Yes, I'm lycan actually and was in the business for ten years before the attack. The law still states we can't treat unaltereds just in case something should happen and we infect them. So here I am. Now... Any preferences?"

"I see. As natural looking as possible and soft to the touch. I was thinking back to the size I was before I lost my weight." She informed nervously.

With a nod, he smiled. "Relax Sarah. While being a therian makes this procedure difficult for my team and I, it's a blessing for you. The pain others suffer for days to weeks, you will only suffer for a few short hours. By the time you leave here, you will be fully healed."

She nodded and smiled.

Then he showed her various products and discussed their pros and cons, and what could and couldn't be done. After a few more questions and answers, they had decided which one to go with and the pricing. She knew the rough price range and was prepared for the worst. However, while he wasn't cheap, he wasn't as expensive as she had been expecting.

"If you have the time, I can do the procedure right now."

"Now? Why is that?" Sarah became suspicious. Even she knew if they were truly good at their job then they would be booked out for weeks if not months. This premise applied for any booking based business as far as she was concerned.

"Being a therian means my only patients are therians or

vampires, I have more spare time than I used to. Therefore, unless the patient doesn't have the time, I'm able to do them when they come in."

"Ah, I see. In that case, yes I have no problems in doing it now." And she relaxed as they continued the consultation.

He then informed her that his team consisted of four others. An anaesthetist at her head, another surgeon and a nurse on one side, with him and another nurse on her other side.

"The reason being is so we can complete the procedure before you metabolise the meds and before you've healed so we won't have to re-open you again."

She nodded her understanding. After phoning the other surgeon and the rest of his team, he explained the procedure to her. Once his team had arrived, they prepped her.

By the time he let her go home, Sarah walked out with natural looking B-cup sized breasts once more. And no pain.

As for the other thing, she decided to wait a while. No particular reason other than she wasn't ready for it at that point in time.

Once her breasts had been done, she went shopping for new clothing. The five outfits that could be mixed and matched just weren't enough. While not that much of a clothes horse, she did like a variety to choose from. Actually, she decided to use it as an excuse to completely overhaul her wardrobe to a style she had been interested in for years.

So, Sarah went a combination of Victorian, Middle Ages, bohemian and corsets with lots of lace, velvet, brocade, chiffon and satin, along with some other lush fabrics. Some of the clothing she decided to make herself and bought a sewing machine as well. She even looked at buying new shoes and accessories to go with her new fashion style.

'I just never went that way because my husband hadn't been interested in seeing me dressed in that style, then when he died I lost interest in just about everything anyway. When I met Danny, I just thought it might have been a bit too clichéd so again I didn't bother. Now, however, I'm free to look the way I want to.'

For the times she had to dress plainly, Sarah decided to stay with what she had bought before going through with the new look. 'Thankfully though, I'm going to keep those sessions to a minimum as much as possible.'

She still kept some standard clothing for the time of the full moon, things that she didn't care if they became ruined. However, after that first time, she decided that darker colours were the way to go so they wouldn't show the blood as easily; such as black, dark blues and dark browns. Red would show up blood very effectively because, once dried, the blood showed up as a brown stain.

For those sorts of clothing, second hand stores became her friends. Cheap and not a drain on the budget when most of them were under five dollars each.

Sarah even changed her hair colour to a brilliant deep red. She had to pre-lighten her original colour first, so she had a fun time of hiding her pre-lightened hair from everyone for that first time until she was ready to colour it the next day. The morning after she had put the red through was an interesting morning.

Those three things she did as a rather late 26th birthday gift to herself even though she never told anyone else when it was her birthday. It wasn't that she was ashamed of her age, far from it, she just hated the fuss of...

"It's my birthday today." In a false cheery voice.

"Oh really? Happy Birthday." Stated in an obligated enthusiastic tone.

'No. I can definitely do without all the obligations. Honestly.'

The day after she put the red in her hair, Sarah was up early sitting in her usual spot at the dining table looking out the window. Her hair was loose so the colour could be clearly seen by those walking up behind her. She heard the first set of footsteps, which sounded like... Mick? perhaps, then they paused, then started walking again but slower than before.

"Wow, Sarah. I mean wow!" Mick said quietly.

"Morning Mick. How are you?" She hid her smile behind her cup of tea.

"Good. Your hair looks amazing."

"Not too over the top?" While she had wanted her hair that colour she just didn't know if it would suit her.

"No, it looks great on you." He said as he sat down with his coffee.

Then she heard Maria and Antonio come out, followed by Toby. Again she hid behind her cup to hide the smile she couldn't stop.

Maria and Antonio didn't say a word. They just walked around the table to stare at her then sat down heavily. They appeared stunned.

"Morning Maria, Ant." She greeted, still hiding behind her cup of tea.

"Morning." They chorused softly, still just staring at her.

Toby, however, had stopped somewhere behind her and hadn't moved.

"Morning Toby." She said while turning around. Then she saw the look on his face. "You don't like it." She said softly.

Even though she had no intention of changing the colour, Sarah was still disappointed that Toby didn't like it. She mentally frowned to herself. 'I don't know why it matters but it does. Toby and I will never be lovers but we are friends and we live under the same roof. So if he doesn't like it then it's going to make things difficult between us.'

"I love it actually. You look awesome Sarah." Toby said quietly sounding more than stunned. He came up to her and gently touched her hair. "You look different and the red hair suits your skin tone... Wow!" his voice was quiet.

For the life of her, she couldn't interpret the expression on his face. She didn't understand why he was behaving the way he was.

"Thank you Toby." She responded softly, hoping to hide her confusion over his reaction.

"I agree with Toby, Luv. You look awesome." Antonio finally stated.

"What made you change your hair colour Honey?" Maria

inquired.

"I've wanted to for years but it never came about. Lately, I've had enough unwanted changes that I decided to have a change of my own choosing." She answered softly. She was feeling a little embarrassed.

For the next few days they kept commenting about it since it was something new. Toby kept giving her strange looks that she couldn't understand. They never talked about it though; even if she did have her suspicions. Something about the expression on his face always stopped her from bringing the subject up and left her feeling rather confused.

When Sarah started wearing her new style of clothing, it sparked off another set of comments.

'Thankfully, they said nice things even though I had asked them to tell me the truth.'

*

It didn't surprise her that no one had noticed her breasts. She had worn clothing baggy enough, and with enough layers, to hide how small they had become due to losing weight. However, she knew Antonio would notice them that night during the next intimacy lesson.

"While I'm surprised about the lack of piercings after our talk Luv, why the breast enhancement?"

She blushed. "I'm a typical female and I did happen to like my breasts before I had lost the weight. I missed them when they disappeared. After what you had said about the piercings, I researched breast implants for therians as well."

She paused and held up her hand when he was about to speak. With an expression of curiosity, he closed his mouth and gave her the time she obviously needed.

"While I wanted the implants, do you think I was wrong?" She whispered nervously.

A smile slowly spread across his lips as he gazed down at her and caressed her nipples then murmured "No Luv. Even an arse man will still enjoy playing with breasts. It was just a surprise. I hadn't even realised you were gone long enough to have them done."

"That was the idea." She murmured as he kissed her.

While she didn't need it, his reaction validated her choice. His reaction also pleased her. With that, the lessons leading up to her second full moon began.

That night, and the following two, were practically the same as the nights before her first full moon. Antonio was there for her no matter what and never criticised her and never was angry with her. He cleaned her up after her partial changes, fed her when they left her too exhausted to even open her eyes, and held her as she soaked in the tub to ease the soreness of her overexerted muscles.

He treated her like a lover and she grew to care for him deeply beyond the friendship they already had. Despite all that, she was still shy. Her shyness amused him and she would smile in spite of herself. And so, that became their routine during those lessons before and after the full moon.

Even the friendship between her and Maria became closer and stronger. It was like the three of them were a family.

~*~

Five and a half weeks after that fateful evening, Kaelan ended up texting Ed to confirm meeting up with him. Since Ed already knew about her, he was the logical person for Kaelan to turn to; despite Ed being the only one he could talk to. Between November the previous year and last month, he and Ed had spoken a few times. Ed, therefore, knew about what had happened to her in October and what came after.

Up until the end of January that was.

They met near the Manly wading pool on the Esplanade again and the day was as miserable as Kaelan felt: low grey clouds and a cool almost cold sea borne wind. Throwing himself into the job had only been partially successful in keeping his mind off her.

Ed was on his feet the moment he saw Kaelan step out of the Jeep. Concern and worry plain on his face. "Kael! What's wrong?"

'Huh, I must look real bad for such an instant reaction from him.' Kaelan couldn't answer at first.

Ed took a step towards him as Kaelan walked over towards the table but then Ed stopped in his tracks. At first he frowned at Kaelan only to replace it with concern again with his mouth and eyes going wide. "Is it Sarah? What's happened to her?"

It surprised Kaelan that Ed thought of her first out of all

the possibilities. 'Am I *that* transparent? God, hopefully only to him.'

For the first time since he was a kid, Kaelan cried and Ed was the only one he could do so in front of. It wasn't that full out blubbering kind of crying but just tears streaming down his face as he sat down at the picnic table and stared out over the choppy water while he tried to regain composure.

"Oh man, I'm sorry. When? Tell me what happened." Ed sounded so devastated for him.

'He's always been free with showing he's still worried about me.'

"Over a month ago but she's not dead." He whispered.

"Oh Kael, don't scare me like that." Ed's shoulders slumped with relief.

"No, she's not dead. She's worse than dead. She's now a therian." Kaelan said, clenching his hands into fists. He never thought he could ever feel that miserable again.

"So she's still alive then?" His friend sounded so relieved.

"Yes."

"Then... why the tears Kael?" Ed now sounded confused.

"Because she's now one of the monsters I hunt for a living and what happened to her is all my fault and she asked a promise from me."

"A promise? *She* got one of your rare promises from you?! Your fault? How was it your fault?" He paused then shook his head. "We'll get through this, just start at the beginning Kael." Ed sounded incredulous, confused and concerned all at once. He sat on the table beside his childhood friend and watched him closely, carefully.

'Never will I understand how Ed manages to feel so many emotions at the same time. But then, he hadn't let himself retreat emotionally from the world like I had.'

That admission surprised Kaelan then he chose to bury it. He was in no way ready for that piece of internal delving. So, starting at the beginning, with when they were last together when he first told Ed about her, to when he saved her life, to when he had destroyed her life.

Ed just sat there and listened as his face became a movie of his feelings and expressions that played across it. Amusement over the little things she did that annoyed his friend. Surprise, disgust and concern in regards to her weight loss programme. Finally, amazement and horror at the hit and attack, then amusement in gaining a promise from his friend, to seriousness over Kaelan having walked away.

By the end of the retelling...

"How do you feel about Sarah the person, Kael?" Ed asked gently.

The question caught Kaelan by surprise and he had to think about it before he could answer.

"I think I love her." He said in shock of such a revelation. He didn't think he had ever admitted that point even privately to himself.

"Then you need to find a way to come to terms with what she is now." Ed paused and peered out over the water for a few moments then looked back at him.

"Ask yourself these two questions Kael... First: has she, as a person, changed from the Sarah you've come to love since becoming a therian? And if the answer is no then, is her being a therian so bad a thing that you can't love her as she is now?" Ed asked in that quiet, point-to-be-made voice of his as he gazed at his friend intently. After a slight pause,

"And the second is, why do you hunt? Is it for revenge, is it for justice and if for justice then whose, or for the thrill of the hunt? You don't have to answer now, but it might help you to know the answers, it might just make your decisions, choices and life in general easier."

Kaelan stared out over the bay as he thought about his friend's questions. 'I'm not really a shallow man but his questions will need a lot of deep thinking; something I haven't done in a long time. Not that deep anyway.'

The two men talked for a while longer before parting ways. To Kaelan, it felt good to talk about her. However, by the time he and Ed went their separate ways, he was still no closer to a solution in regards to her.

Chapter 9

It was the night of the full moon. The last three nights of the lessons of control were like last month; partial changes and painful. When Sarah woke up that afternoon and met with everyone in the kitchen, she looked at Maria and Antonio. "What are the plans for tonight?"

"We'll be socialising at Jonathon's again. Basically a repeat of last month." Maria answered.

She looked down at her hands then back up at them. "Do we have to go there tonight?" She asked tentatively.

"Why Luv? What's wrong?" Antonio frowned with concern obvious in his voice.

"Ummm... Please don't take this the wrong way, but Jonathon's gatherings seem to be just too formal and I don't feel right when I'm there." Sarah could feel herself turning red by the heat that crept over her face.

"Did you have anywhere else in mind? We need somewhere that isn't going to scare the general populace." Antonio asked.

With just a nod of her head Sarah indicated to the view out the window. They turned and gazed at it in surprise. To top off the suggestion, a deer could be seen foraging at the tree line before something spooked it and it disappeared into the bush land that occupied the back of the property. "Plus, the neighbours aren't that close."

When she had first seen the deer in the back yard, she had asked Kaelan about them. He had said it was because his parents had liked them.

"I'll go let Jonathon know that we won't be there tonight." Antonio said with a smile.

"Thank you." She smiled in relief. "I think I'm going to have to restock the deer though." She blushed as she hadn't thought of that before.

While Antonio made the call, Maria grinned. "We'll give you the name and number of a supplier."

"That would be great, thank you."

"Well, he wasn't too happy that I wouldn't be there, but he said I had to be there tomorrow." He peered at Sarah. "Maria and I have never been separated since we became leopards."

"I would never dream of separating you pair during this time. If you need to go to Jonathon's then we'll go."

"No, it's already organised. We don't have to go to his place tonight."

"Thank you Ant." Sarah was relieved. Jonathon was okay but too stuffy and formal for her. Just because she was now a therian, it hadn't changed what she thought about him. 'I don't know, he always seems condescending and looking down his nose at people.'

"Sarah, would you mind if I invited a few others?" Maria

asked.

"No, go right ahead. It'll make it more fun. What if we did a barbecue for light eating? We have enough for... say... Six people in total, without having to go out and buy extra. We have the barbecue early evening and then the hunt tonight. Toby and Mick are leaving shortly and won't be back until three days' time."

"Sounds good. Are you up to playing hostess this soon?" Antonio asked.

"Only one way to find out." She said with a smile and a shrug. "I'm only sorry about the small number of people we can cater to, but I think I need small numbers right now. I found last month rather overwhelming."

"Don't let it upset you Dear. Not everyone can handle big gatherings and Jonathon never does anything on a small scale." Maria said.

"I've noticed."

With that, they started preparations for the food and started cleaning the house and the barbecue. By early evening everything was organised and set up with table and chairs down near the pool. The three guests arrived at that point. The first two were Candy and Preston, whom Sarah had never met before.

Candy looked like a swimsuit model, curves in all the right places and tanned. However, her skin was too smooth that made Sarah thought her tan wasn't by the sun. Her bottle blonde hair was just past her shoulders. She had hazel eyes that sparkled with inner amusement.

Preston also looked like he could have been a model, well build, great tan, light brown hair with light green eyes that bordered on hazel. They were lovers with no plans in getting married.

The third person to arrive was Luke. While she wasn't surprised, she sort of was at the same time.

'What is it with my friends? Are they all trying to match-make me with someone or what?'

As it was he'd pretty much attached himself to Sarah for the night. She was polite but tried to make sure she didn't look like she was coming on to him. A very difficult balance to achieve.

The evening was a nice light hearted event. They laughed, partook of the barbecue, told stories, Maria and Antonio encouraged the others to nag Sarah into playing the keyboard and sing. So she did about an hours' worth, with the singing first. Placing a cd in the stereo, the first song was *'Give Me Head'* by The Radiators.

"Oh no. I'm not singing that one." She exclaimed in mortification.

The rest teased her and sang parts of it themselves as they laughed and joked.

"...Gimme head like you did just last night..." Minus Sarah.

"...Each time I see you I grow weak at the knees

You sink me under, bring me undone

With words you said, words you said"

Sarah blushed and laughed and sang the odd part or two.

"but best of all, all those you gimme head" Again without Sarah.

After the music and fun, they ended the night by shifting form, hunting a deer and consuming it, then paired off – Sarah with Luke of course – for the grooming session. They fell asleep under the trees and changed back to human form as they slept. Come morning, they wandered back to the house to clean up and have breakfast.

Yes, Sarah did wake up naked beside an equally naked Luke again. Once again, he assured her nothing but cleaning happened between them. She just couldn't stop being embarrassed about it, however. Yet, in the back of her mind was always that niggling speck of doubt, because she just didn't know. After the feast, she had no memory of what happened afterward. Antonio told her later that her memory of those sessions would improve as time went by.

Also, and to be expected, Luke commented on her breast enhancements. She gave him the same reason she'd told Antonio while blushing profusely. He grinned, helped her up and they headed back to the house.

One thing Sarah had discovered was that her fur was a creamy white with ever so slightly darker cream coloured rosettes that shimmered somewhat whenever she moved. She was a white were-jaguar. The only information she could find was that real white jaguars were truly rare, let alone the normal jaguars, outside the Americas. Apparently the one whom attacked her was the first in Australia and that she had been in the country illegally anyway.

By the end of the second full moon session Sarah was back at work with a full work day. She was also glad her own nails were starting to look good again. All her current clients had seen her new website and liked the idea of having their nails done by a therian.

It was beside the point her web site said they would never see her change due to work place health and safety and other legalities. To cover herself legally Sarah had working security cameras installed and bought new discs each week. She then wrote the date, with start and finish times, on them and stored them should they ever be needed.

The reason why was because working with the Therian League, before she became a therian herself, she got to hear about accusations against therians. With no proof of innocence, let alone guilt, some of the therians had been executed before it was discovered that the human involved had lied.

However, her days went well and her appointment book full during her chosen hours. Although, she did refuse to work during the full moon.

*

By the late half of March – after her intimacy lessons, Sarah decided it was time to deal with the house up at Caboolture. Before anything could be done about it, everything in regards to it had to be documented; both on paper and with photographs. She took time off work to take inventory and photos so she knew exactly what was there.

First, she packed all of Abel's and Brandi's personal belongings. During the process she found documents with whom the house and property was insured with. She rang them and asked if they could send someone out after she had explained all that had happened in October past.

It took almost three weeks to record everything inside and out, with the library taking the longest. No, Sarah hadn't sat there reading while recording. Reason being, she wanted to be out of the house as quickly as possible. Emotionally, she just couldn't handle being constantly swamped with the memories of them and the tears. By the end of each day she was exhausted; physically and emotionally.

Then, finally, it was all done.

Lastly, she set about getting the yard, gardens and pool back into their original condition. To do that, she organised a landscaper and a pool guy; both who were willing to work for a therian. Actually, the landscaper was easy; she hired Antonio.

After showing him photographs Brandi and Abel had taken, she had fun helping him; following his instructions. Also, at his suggestion, she updated the watering system and included some low maintenance weed eliminating solutions.

Ever since she had inherited the house, Sarah had been debating with herself as to what to do with it. She didn't know whether to keep it, sell it or rent it; regardless of her earlier decision to not sell. By the time she had finished bringing the house and property back to its former glory, she decided to keep it as a get-away; even if she still couldn't handle being around it just yet. She couldn't bear the thought of anyone else living in it.

She did, however, pay for regular yard and pool

maintenance. Who she hired for regular yard maintenance was at Antonio's suggestion.

*

The next two months were a repeat of the first two months. Sarah was so over the pain of the partial changes. She hated them so much that she was dreading the lead-up to the full moon. By the end of her third full moon in April, Maria and Antonio moved back to their own home with Antonio coming round to take her out for her intimacy lessons.

While by the fourth full moon, she had even taken to avoiding Luke.

'I'm just not interested in him that way. Oh, he's attractive enough, rather nice personality and sense of humour, but no matter how hard I try my heart belongs to someone else.'

Maria and Antonio asked her if there was anything wrong between Luke and her. She just told them no, that she loved someone else. That comment earned her a strange look from them. Sarah had guessed it was to be expected since they didn't really see her with anyone else.

However, she didn't know what else to do. She did try to be interested in Luke but it didn't work out that way. But how does one explain being in love with someone who's never around, who more than likely doesn't return that love? Sarah knew she couldn't.

She also spent one of those full moons at Jonathon's and it was just as boring as before. In the end she managed to avoid his gatherings every second or third session. However, she couldn't avoid him totally.

Unfortunately, by her reckoning, she had to become involved in the political side of things. Being the only jaguar around, she had to speak up for herself. So, she just stated how she felt about something regardless of whether her opinion agreed with Jonathon's or not; let alone anyone else's. She had even managed to irritate him a few times because of her opinions.

If she could stay out of that side of therian affairs then she would. Give her a straight voting and she's fine. But those discussions, where Jonathon tried to brow beat those who disagreed with him into changing their minds and swing his way, were tedious. In fact, she suspected that was why he held those discussions; just to make sure he got his own way. She refused to let him change her mind.

Sarah had to admit to herself that she was surprised as well that she was able to stand up for herself like that. She was still nervous as ever – the butterflies alive and well and still without a net – but if she disagreed then she said so. She wasn't the only one surprised by her newly discovered backbone. The first time Maria and Antonio heard her disagree with Jonathon their mouths hung open then they grinned, having to hide their smiles from him.

Her choosing to disagree with Jonathon encouraged others to do so as well. Without him being able to change their minds on the subject irritated him immensely. Whenever it happened, he gave Sarah very dirty looks to say it was all her fault. However, she wouldn't change her opinions just to please him.

The latest meeting had been such a drag as far as Sarah was concerned. Jonathon deliberately dragged it out with his typical brow beating and semi subtle verbal bullying as he tried to swing some of the decisions back to what he wanted. She tried to appear normal as she sat there in a mixture of boredom, frustration and wanting to cry. While he left her alone during this particular session, the poisonous daggers being shot her way from him hadn't lessened.

"What do you think Sarah?" Rick a newly relocated were-fox asked her. His lovely grey eyes revealed the pressure he was feeling by Jonathon's intimidation.

"Don't ask her! She is but one voice. You know what I'm saying is right. Just damned well agree." Jonathon shouted angrily. The veins at his temples looked like they were going to burst.

Sarah noted the shocked expressions from Antonio and Maria, as well as a few others, over his outburst. She closed her eyes and tried to take a calming breath but it didn't help the churning in her gut these sessions created within her.

"I don't agree this is the way we should go without refining the proposal some more but that is just my opinion." She stated softly, hoping the last would pacify Jonathon.

"Don't agree?! You haven't given one valid reason for not agreeing to the proposal!" Jonathon shouted at her yet again. So much for pacification.

Another quick glance at those around the table and Sarah could see the disbelief over his statement in their eyes. She slumped wearily in her seat. He was deliberately dragging the situation out longer than necessary in the attempt to get the others to swing back his way.

Five minutes later Jonathon angrily called the meeting to an end and dismissed everyone. As they all rose to leave…

"Sarah, stay for a minute." His voice was low but she could hear the strain underlining his tone.

Sitting back down, she watched as the others left and her nervousness rose. As Maria and Antonio passed her, their eyes briefly met hers before they too left the room. Once the doors to the meeting room closed there was a few moments pause then…

"What the hell do you think you are doing? Every time I put forward things for the good of the community, you continually go against me. Why do you keep challenging my authority in public like this? I have had enough of your behaviour and will not tolerate it any longer." He wasn't exactly shouting but his voice wasn't calm and quiet either.

She opened her mouth to speak, but before she could utter a word in her defence his eyes narrowed with what seemed like suspicion and maybe hatred.

"Are you challenging me personally? Do you want to take control of everything I have worked hard to build and strive for, is that it?" He demanded, his voice becoming louder and louder.

Again, before she could say anything…

"How dare you, you ungrateful little bitch! You are nothing but a weak child. You had not even started high school by the time I became leader of the lepe and the therian league. You're not even old enough as a therian to be classified as responsible.

How dare you challenge me when you owe me for your very existence. If it wasn't for me you would be lost and alone. If it wasn't for me accepting you into my clan you would have nothing..." He yelled at her as he attempted to tower over her from his side of the table, trying to intimidate her.

She had enough and shot to her feet.

"Yes it's true you accepting me into the lepe helped me when I needed it and in no way am I ungrateful for it. I'm not interested in wanting control over the lepe or the league. I never have been. Surely you can't believe that just because I disagree with you if I happen to think you're wrong." She made the mistake of pausing to collect her thoughts for the rest she wanted to say.

"Wrong?! You are so naive that you wouldn't know what is right or wrong in these matters." He roared at her as he slammed his hands done on the table in anger.

Tears welled in her eyes as the entire situation became too much for her. She started to shake ever so slightly as she stated, "If you want me to leave the clan and manage by myself then I'll do it. However, after what the others have witnessed here today, they might think you're afraid of me if I do, and that would look bad for you. Honestly, you have nothing to fear from me. I am not interested in leadership of any kind. I've only been voicing my opinion."

Even though the tears could be heard in her voice, they hadn't started falling. Yet. She dared not to blink or look down or they would fall, but it was so hard for her to fight her natural instinct to look down at her feet.

He paused momentarily. Then, with a snarl, he swept the

papers of the table in frustration.

"Get out!" He growled at her as he kept himself leaning over the table with his hands planted flat upon it. It seemed to her like he was deliberately stopping himself from lunging at her to kill her.

Quickly grabbing her bag and walking stick, Sarah gratefully rushed out of the room. She was also grateful no one was in the corridor waiting as she hobbled as fast as she could out the front door as the tears finally started to fall. On the front landing to the door, she literally ran into Antonio and Maria. Since the middle of the meeting, she had forgotten she had come with them and not on her scooter.

"Sarah? Luv? Are you okay? Did he hurt you?" Antonio asked anxiously as both he and Maria wrapped their arms around her.

"N-no. He was just pissed o-off because I've been standing up to him every time." She sobbed as she tried to calm herself.

"I know he was angry but I didn't think it was enough for him to ream you for it." Maria stated in mild exasperation.

Since Sarah was gazing up at Antonio after bumping into him, she saw his frown at her comment then the rise of his eyebrows at his wife's comment. Then he reached up to wipe her tears away.

"He does need to learn to deal with it better that's for sure." He paused then grinned down at her. "However, you standing up to him like that at each of the meetings has definitely been a surprise. Let's get out of here."

And they left, with them inviting her out to dinner where they demanded all the details from her.

*

It was the beginning of June, the first month of winter and rather cold; windy as well. When it rained it was freezing. It didn't snow in Brisbane. The lead up to her fifth full moon started to show some improvements. She still did the partial change during the lessons but it wasn't as painful. Nor was it as severe with the contortions. The extent of the partial changes were also less as it seemed to be restricting itself to just her hands. Her changes during the full moon were also becoming less painful. Either that or she was becoming used to them.

Sarah pretty much kept to herself, mingling with other therians when she couldn't avoid it. Every time she had to mingle, Luke was there and, finally, he cornered her.

"What have I done Sarah? Why are you avoiding me?" He seemed hurt over her actions and she realised she had to explain to him.

"Let's walk." She said softly and when they were far enough away that no one could hear them she turned to him.

"I'm sorry Luke. I never meant to hurt you. You're attractive, kind, wonderful, plus a number of other things. You haven't done anything wrong. You see... I'm in love with another man and I avoided you so you wouldn't get the wrong idea. I didn't realise... I just didn't realise. I'm sorry." Her voice faded to nothing as she stared at her feet.

"And you want to be just friends?" He sounded rather neutral.

"I can't help how I feel." She whispered. Damn it, but she couldn't stop the tears.

Luke walked away. From that moment on he avoided her. It was that extra push for her to cut yet another tie that was keeping her mingling with the lepe.

Sarah went further into the darkness to cry then, going around the outside of the house to avoid everyone else, hopped on her scooter and left. She rode around for a while, going out to Fisherman's Island – doing the loop there, then out to the Wynnum-Manly area and parked in a parking bay opposite the southern end of the park that was nestled between Upper Esplanade and Lower Esplanade, to just stare out to sea.

She tried not to think, but as per usual, it never really worked out. She thought about Luke and how hurt he'd sounded.

'I didn't think I'd led him on. I hadn't meant to hurt him.'

She felt so bad about it that the tears started welling again. Then she thought about Kaelan, wondering what he was doing right then and how much she missed him, and the tears flowed freely down her face.

'How have I managed to stuff up so badly when I wasn't even really doing anything?'

Sarah tried to think what she could have done differently. She supposed there was plenty she could have done differently but just couldn't see them right then. She didn't have an answer and the tears kept falling. The winds off the sea were very chilly as they dried the tears on her cheeks and she huddled into her jacket.

She hoped Luke would find it in his heart to forgive her some day and hoped to hear from Kaelan, no matter how hard she tried not to think about him.

Wiping her tears away, she headed home.

~*~

As the months went by, Kaelan read the reports as they came in. Some of the information he expected. Others he hadn't. His property hosting therian gatherings at the time of the full moon was one he hadn't been expecting. One particular skinny male therian who always seemed to be starkers whenever he was with her was another.

It was beside the point others around her were naked as well because they never walked out of the bushland at the back of his property with her close beside them. She, however, seemed to be dressed every time.

His mouse suddenly cracked in his hand and he let go of it as if it had burnt or sliced him. He stared at the device in shock as a realisation hit him like a bullet between the eyes.

'I'm jealous!' Due to his own beliefs, and continuing absence, he knew he had no reason to be but he was. He couldn't recall ever being jealous before.

Kaelan walked away from his laptop before the alien feeling caused him to kill it as well. Taking a breather, he went out and bought two new mouses; just in case. It was bad enough to admit to Ed he loved her but to experience jealousy as well?

"She is so going to be the death of me! I just know it!" He

growled to himself.

Once a new mouse was connected he went back to reading the reports...

After around the fifth or sixth month she and the skinny therian seemed to stop hanging out together.

'Had they been lovers and had a lovers tiff? No info came through in that regard other than they were never seen behaving like lovers. The pair of them could have kept their... relationship a secret I guess.'

So he had no way of knowing if they were or weren't. Again, the reports kept saying she acted as if she wasn't involved with him. However, he now felt like a fool for being jealous over something which might never have been.

'How the hell has she managed to up-end my world so badly?!' He shook he head, absolutely clueless.

He was pleased to read Mick and Toby were still with her and looking after her. Not only were the 2IC and his wife living in his house for almost three months before leaving, but Antonio and Sarah have been seen on what looked like dates – evenings out – days before and after the full moon since her first month.

To him, it appeared as if they were dating. 'But if so, then why only immediately before and after the full moon?'

For what reason for both pieces of information, Kaelan had no idea and his informants were unable to gather any more specifics about their circumstances. He found the situation frustrating. Pushing back from the table, he sat back in the chair, clasped his hands behind his head and frowned at the laptop.

'How the hell can I work things out if my informants can't obtain all the relevant details?!'

Chapter 10

The months went by, sometimes seemingly quickly and sometimes seemingly slow. Winter gave way to spring and spring gave way to summer with Christmas less than three weeks away. Luke never forgave Sarah and stayed away from her. While she never heard from Kaelan at all since he had left. On that front her life was a mess.

Sometime during August or September she heard rumours of there being more jaguars in Brisbane. Due to her private life, her therian lessons and her business she didn't do anything about trying to find out about them or to meet them. Sarah was only interested in keeping herself afloat with all that was and wasn't happening in her life. She didn't need to add more therian politics into her life; even if they were of her species.

However, due to the therian meetings, she did see some there. Still, she didn't go out of her way to get to know them and they didn't come near her.

Her lessons of control during intimacy came to an end during the first month of spring. Seven months after becoming a therian, she was finally able to control the partial changes. Sarah was immensely grateful when she could. It was difficult for her to explain the difference between control and fighting the change, so she tried by writing it down; just to help it become clearer in her own mind...

Fighting the change is where the change is happening but the therian is trying to stop it from happening by tensing to prevent movement. Controlling the change is learning to control ones feelings, emotions, desires before the change starts to happen, thereby hopefully preventing the change from starting. Once it starts to happen the therian must then relax. While not always successful, the relaxation can sometimes reverse the change. If not, then it won't – shouldn't - hurt as much if the therian stays relaxed.

...She closed the notebook with a sigh.

Antonio, Maria and Sarah discovered Sarah could do partial changes on her hands without changing the rest of herself. Antonio could do it as well, but Maria couldn't. It's not a rare ability per se, but it wasn't common either.

"I should have realised due to how quickly you heal. We've worked out, at least, that fast healing and being an alpha do seem to go hand in hand." Antonio then told her it started placing her higher in the ranks and the only thing holding her back was a lack of strength and the ability to fight.

And, maybe, a lack of ambition. In reality, Sarah wasn't that worried about it. She wasn't interested in rising in the ranks at all. If the other therians left her alone she would be a very happy kitty.

"I suggest we three keep this information between ourselves. Reason why I suggest this is so people will underestimate you Sarah, and so you won't receive power-based challenges." Maria advised.

"Good idea, Gattina." Antonio smiled at his wife as Sarah nodded. Sarah smiled slightly and glanced away at his endearment of kitten in Italian.

All in all, Sarah was pleased with the way her life was going for a change. Her life was starting to settle into a regular routine.

'Well, almost pleased, if it wasn't for Luke and Kaelan. But ignoring them, my life is good. My changes are smoother, my partials are a lot less painful and my business is doing well. So well in fact that I've started remodelling inside so I can employ staff. Heh... I'm going from a home business to a true business.'

A year after the death of her friends, after deciding upon the expansion to her business, she had to buy extra furniture to accommodate the extra staff; as well as buying extra equipment for each table. Standard table lamps, uv lamps, files, buffers, tips, acrylic – even though she's been thinking about excluding it in the near future, gels, etc. All of it cost a fortune but was worth it. When Sarah had started her own business she never thought she would be turning it into a business with employees.

So, she was looking at employing seven staff; three for day time with her and four for evening because she didn't want to work evenings any more. Therefore, in the weeks that followed

Sarah met with applicants of all kinds... male and female; human, therian and vampires.

She ended up employing three males and four females: two vampires, a therian and four humans. They had to be chosen carefully as she wanted them all to be able to work with each other. Since the therian and the vampires were all registered, Sarah and her new staff announced what they were on the website, along with the updated hours and who would be working when.

Sarah's nightshift staff consisted of: Night manager Benjamin (Ben or Benji) Taylor who was a vampire. Helena Carlson, the other vampire, was second in charge whenever Benjamin wasn't there. Waneta Zanthier who happened to be were-wolf, and last member of the night team was a human called Graham Noley.

The rest of Sarah's daytime staff were all human: Petra Lantan became her second in charge if Sarah should happen to not be there. Nate Carter and Lucy Ashton were the other two techs who completed her daytime crew.

Sarah chose them for their skills, which were similar to her own. She chose her night manager and seconds based on past management skills, and the three men seemed happy that she had employed them.

'I like the idea of male nail techs. They're good, as well as good for business. There should be more of them actually.' She thought with a smile.

However, all meetings had to be held an hour after sunset to give the vampires a chance to arrive at the nail bar. Other than that, it was business as usual.

~*~

A brief deviation in the reports told him Brisbane had a new vampire Prince of the City who had only been in the country for six months before killing the previous Prince and claiming the title. He had heard rumours the previous Prince was savage and he was somehow linked to the disappearance of some women. No proof could be found though; despite the suggestion being as the reason for the newcomer's attack. Since the reign of the new Prince, only good words have been spoken by those who keep the peace and balance between the monsters and the humans. The new Prince seemed to be against harming humans, unless in self-defence, and especially just for feeding.

Kaelan reserved the right to make a judgement until more information came in.

Back to Sarah...

She'd expanded her business to include staff now and seemed to be an almost 24hr business. She's employed a mix of humans, therians and vamps as well as a mix of males and females. Her business now boasted four nail techs (including herself) during the day and four techs operating at night. He visited her nail bar website and read all info there.

It surprised him to see her website matched the theme of her shop. It pleased him immensely as that told him she liked the decor he had chosen. Amazingly, her business was booming even with the new staff. It seemed vamps now had a decent place to go to and normal people seemed to like the idea of therians and/or vamps doing their nails. Kaelan supposed it was a good thing really since she herself is a therian. Regardless, he just stared at her website. He had no idea how take the news that his land now hosted the monsters on a daily basis.

While he looked forward to those reports, what he couldn't stand was when they'd tell him 'the rumours have it...'. The latest rumour stated she was stirring the pot within the therian league by disagreeing with Sutterton, the league's chair person. Apparently it wouldn't be such a big deal except it seemed other, smaller voices, were adding theirs to hers and therefore disagreeing with him as well. It appeared to be all because of her.

He found the reports unbelievable. She was too much of a scared baby bunny – revenge not included – to stand up to someone like Sutterton. Sutterton was a rich cultured bully-boy and didn't like it when others went against his way of thinking. Kaelan had heard the man brow beats the smaller voices until they voted his way. However, it seemed, not any more since she had started participating.

'I look forward to more reports about this little outcome.' He mused.

~*~

Just when things were settling down into some semblance of normality, Sarah's little part of the world upended itself yet again. At first what had happened didn't affect her, but after the dust had settled then she was flipped like a pancake.

Christmas came and went and turned out to be a non-event for her. Toby and Mick spent it with their girlfriends or with whoever they chose and wherever else they wanted to be, which wasn't at home. So, Sarah spent it alone after telling Antonio and Maria a little lie that she would be spending it elsewhere with other people. She also spent the New Year alone. She just wanted some alone time for a change. While things between her and Jonathon weren't getting any worse, they weren't getting any better either. For the time being at least.

During the month of Christmas there was a change in the city's leadership within the vampire community. The head – called a Prince regardless of gender – vampire lost a battle for control of the city to a newly arrived vampire. As one could see, that didn't affect Sarah at all. However, just after the New Year, the new Prince decided to take a liking to her and to let her know it. Again, that normally wouldn't be a big problem.

The problem was that the new Prince was a woman and her animal to call was the jaguar. While Sarah was a jaguar, she wasn't into women as a lover. To top it off, the rumour was now fact that Sarah was no longer the only jaguar in Brisbane; the Prince came with some in her entourage. The new prince also came with other vampires and some humans. The first thing she discovered about them was that the new prince and her entourage were Americans. While she suspected the jags were, it was a surprise that the prince and the rest of her crew were.

Thinking it wouldn't be long before she would be dragged into their politics, Sarah decided to do a bit of general vampire research...

Vampires have the ability to mesmerise with their eyes; this Sarah already knew. They can change into any predator creature they want; if they're powerful enough. If they are powerful enough, with the right teacher – as in their sire, then they may be able to have an animal to call. If they have an animal to call then all of that species can't refuse the call. The natural animals definitely can't, however, the therian versions can if they are strong enough. But there are rarely any of the real animals around in Australia except what might be in zoos.

When the call goes out it feels like a compulsion, a tugging on a line one never realised was there. The first time she felt 'the call', she didn't know what it was. Not until she had read about it. Afterwards, whenever Sarah felt that tugging, it took a lot of effort to refuse it. While there had been numerous calls, the first seriously strong one she couldn't refuse and found herself standing in front of the Prince. That was just weeks after the new prince gained her position.

The woman in front of Sarah was taller than her – a regular occurrence with Sarah being so short – with an olive complexion and features that reminded her more of a Native North American than any other race. Wearing a light tan coloured tailored pants suit and appeared to almost mimic a Native American outfit. She had straight dark brown hair that brushed her waist as she moved. Sarah thought her eyes were brown but wasn't sure as she refused to look the Prince in the eyes after that first quick glance, which the woman found highly amusing.

The Prince appeared to be about Sarah's age, but since she

was a vampire it was an irrelevant point. To become a Prince of the city she was either very good for a young age – unlikely, or she's much older. Like over a hundred at least, to be powerful enough to defeat the previous Prince. Sarah was guessing the vampire to be over a hundred.

"Do you know who I am?" Like Sarah's, her voice was deep but deeper than the therian's, deeper than she was expecting. However, unlike Sarah, her voice sounded amazing, like something for good phone sex. Smooth, rich while her own sounded rather rough and grating to her own ears.

"Other than you're the new Prince of the City, your animal to call is jaguar and have seen you around on the odd occasion, no." She refused to look the Prince in the eyes at all.

"I am Orenda. I have seen you around and noted you answered my calls so I knew you were a jaguar." She said smugly.

"I've never answered your calls." Sarah frowned at the woman with a small shake of her head then remembered those invisible tugs she had experienced.

"Every time you saw me, you were responding to my calls. However, it seems you are the only other jaguar here, other than my entourage." She responded with an indication at the men with her and a self-satisfied smile.

Sarah regarded the two men; one on either side of the Prince. Both were Native American in appearance, roughly the same height with brown eyes and dark brown hair. Both of them stood there looking strong and proud, but not in an arrogant way. She recognised them for the warriors they were. Not only that, but both were rather attractive, however, that was where the similarities ended.

The one on Sarah's left was slim like a long distance runner, dressed like a Native North American Indian. In what looked like long doe skin pants with matching moccasins, but no shirt, she realised his clothing were similar in colour to the Prince's suit. Then, she noted his hair was down to his waist with a narrow braid down one side at the front. All that was missing was the war paint, headband and feather.

Sarah knew her description sounded clichéd but that was the way he was dressed. She didn't know that much about Native American Indians and therefore couldn't tell if he was being clichéd or it was his people's original style.

As for the one on her right: he was stockier, broader in the chest and shoulders but not fat, just a more solid build and hair just as long but with no braid. His clothing was Native South American; as in Aztec, Mayan, Incan... She knew even less about them than she did the Native North American Indians.

He wore a cape instead of a shirt, but had on a sort of skirt – but not a skirt, like a fancy breechcloth but was sure it had a particular name – that left his thighs bare instead of pants and was wearing a pair of sandals that one would never be able to buy from local or specialty shoe stores. He looked impressive; as did his thighs. Very impressive.

Sarah frowned. She so didn't need the added complication of another attraction. As far as she was concerned both looked hot and yummy but the stockier one affected her inside and the feeling stayed there whether she was looking at him or not. Even when she wasn't looking at him, she was very much aware of him.

Their eyes met and she saw a... hunger, for lack of a better word, in his eyes that he didn't even bother trying to hide from her. It seemed to be a look that was just for her. 'Or maybe I'm just reading too much into his expression.'

"These are two of my jaguars. The one on your left is Anoki (pronounced Ah-no-key) and the one on your right is Itztecpatl. The two of them have been with me the longest out of all my jaguars." She said proudly.

With a name like that, the one on the left confirmed her suspicions regarding his nationality. While the name of the one on the right just confused her as to which was his nationality. In that moment, she decided to think of him as the Aztec.

When the Prince had mentioned the one and only jaguar who resided in Brisbane over a week earlier, that person's presence in Australia was an immensely unexpected surprise to Itztecpatl. He had thought they were the first. Finally, he got his first good look at the jaguar. He was surprised to see it was a young woman. Before the meeting, Orenda hadn't mentioned the gender and he had assumed it was a guy since there were more male were-jaguars than females.

Dressed in a blue and green tartan checked ankle length skirt with a black knit three quarter sleeved top and black slip-on shoes, she was tiny. No more than five one or five two at the most. Her skin was as fair as his was dark and was slim of build which was typical of their kind. She was very feminine looking as if she didn't work out in a gym at all and he thought she would therefore be easy to bring into line under their rules.

She had waist length red hair but it seemed to be coloured,

not natural but still striking, and eyes that seemed to be the greyish-blue colour of storm clouds. Other than that she was rather plain to look at. Except for her lips. Her lips, while not thick and full, were luscious just the same with its cute little cupid's bow and painted in a berry coloured lipstick.

He noted her disability that had to have happened before becoming a jaguar. She had to walk with a walking stick which had a figurehead of a crouching, snarling white panther of some sort.

'Could it be a reference to the colourisation of her spirit? Or is it just a coincidence?'

It surprised him greatly that her voice was a little deeper than he had been expecting; although, not as deep as the Prince's. Also surprisingly she was Australian, not American like he had been expecting.

The first time young woman gazed at Anoki and him, and their eyes met, Itztecpatl saw he would have to work at bringing her into line.

'She may be little in height but I can see the fire in her eyes and I know I will enjoy teaching her who is in charge. Oh, I would never hurt her in any way as that just isn't my style. However, I have always loved a challenge and I think she will be one enjoyable challenge indeed.'

"Nice for them. Why have you called me here?" Sarah was nervous, she didn't like being summoned the way she had been. And, dealing with that subject allowed her to ignore the other standing at the Prince's side.

'She's afraid.' Itztecpatl noted that fact with surprise.

"Because I like you, attracted to you, so pretty and want you with me. Why so nervous Kitten?" She sounded truly curious as to why, but that first comment sounded like what one says to their lover.

'I am so not going there.' Sarah thought to herself.

Itztecpatl knew Orenda was a lover of women and he normally didn't have a problem with it but this time he was annoyed. He was surprised that it annoyed him because he didn't even know the young woman standing in front of them, but for some reason she mattered to him.

He had to fight to keep from frowning, to keep his expression neutral as he didn't need to experience Orenda's anger.

"I'm a very shy person and I don't deal well with other people. A woman as my lover is so not my thing. I also don't like having been summoned against my will like this." Still Sarah refused to look the Prince in the face. She didn't know if the vampire would use mind control on her or if she would be able to fight it. Either way, she didn't want to find out.

It pleased him immensely to hear the young woman say she wasn't a lover of women. There were certainly more than enough bi-sexual and gay women in Orenda's court without another one added to the mix. He continued to watch her intently even though she barely looked away from Orenda's general direction. He was also pleased to see she was smart by not looking into Orenda's eyes. If she did, he didn't think she would be able to refuse Orenda anything.

"You are not a lover of women? Such a shame. Look me in the eyes little kitty." She ordered.

Sarah felt the tug of that order but she fought it, "No!" The word came out strained and took some effort as she stubbornly kept her eyes on the Prince's throat and chin. Vampire mind control required eye contact so Sarah knew that wasn't what she was experiencing.

'Is this part of her animal to call?' Her fear jumped up a notch or two.

Itztecpatl stood there and watched, reserving his opinion about her as very few had ever refused Orenda's call. No matter how hard they tried. He could most of the time but not all of the time.

"Look me in the eyes and come to me." Her voice was more insistent this time.

While not to the same extent as the young woman before him, even he could feel it.

Sarah took a step forward, fighting it. "No!" She said again through clenched teeth and fought to take that one step back. She was sure it wasn't pretty, but she did it. It took a lot of effort that she had sweat trickling down her back and temples.

'I can grow to hate this woman very easily and very quickly.' Sarah thought sourly.

He watched her perspiring, in fighting to take that one step back. It was a struggle, but she did it and it was amazing to see.

'This one is strong, and with such fire within her. Seems I have a challenge ahead of me in taming her. I'm so looking forward to it.' He fought to keep a lid on his excitement.

"A strong little kitty. And does this little kitty have claws as well?" The Prince sounded amused.

"Come and find out." She stated then looked sort of horrified at what she had just said.

'What the fudging hell had I just said?! I can't believe I just said that.' Sarah didn't want the woman anywhere near her.

Watching her, he thought that little revelation of her reaction to her own comment was amusing. 'I would think... she is the cautious type... until she's pushed a little too far for her reckoning then she will say something that's not typical for her, only to be shocked by what she's said and/or done. Unfortunately with no way to retract what she's said she ends up finding herself between a rock and a hard place.'

'The question is, what will this cornered little kitty do? I guess I'm about to find out.'

She saw the Prince flick her hand and the one called Anoki started to come towards her. She held her left hand away from her side and let it change into claws. Anoki stopped where he was and gazed back at Orenda.

'An alpha!' Itztecpatl's astonished thoughts exclaimed.

'There will be no taming of this one after all, but can I dominate her? It will be interesting to find out. Is that why I'm attracted to her? That my spirit recognised hers before I did? I will have to get to know this little fire kitty.'

"Well, well. Our little kitty here is an Alpha. What a prize I have in you."

'Yes, Orenda would see her as a prize.' He thought bitterly.

"I'm no one's prize and definitely not yours. If you called me here for games then I'm leaving." Sarah didn't get the chance to turn around when Orenda motioned Itztecpatl forward.

'If I can read her nervousness then so can Orenda.'

Since the ground was level, Sarah laid the walking stick down and changed her right hand into claws as well, but he kept coming towards her. His hands were human normal still.

Slowly, he kept going towards her. While he too could change just his hands, he didn't want to hurt her just yet so he let his hands stay as they were. 'Besides, my reach is longer than hers so once I grab her by the arms she won't be able to hurt me.'

'Maybe he can't do partial changes or he doesn't want to hurt me. Here's hoping either way.'

His plan would have worked if the young woman hadn't stepped into his reaching hands. It had been unexpected. The move placed her closer to him so she swiped him up his chest from left hip to right shoulder just as his hands gripped her upper arms. Two things happened almost at the same time.

He hissed in pain.

When he touched her something, neither of them sure what exactly, that felt like an electrical shock passed between them and their beasts started to rise as if the two of them were going to change. Both could sense the shifting in each other. While the scratches she gave him did hurt, he could feel they were superficial only. While Sarah didn't understand how she could be sensing his beast at all.

The second thing was he let go of her as soon as she had swiped him a scoring blow, minimal damage that looked worse than it really was, so the contact between them was barely a second or two. They both staggered backwards.

Sarah from whatever it was that passed between them and him from that same something and the slashing she had given him. She was having a difficult time trying to breathe. Sarah stared at him and he appeared to be having the same problem and she didn't think it had to do with the scratches she had just given him. They frowned at each other.

'Had she felt it as well?' He stared at her as she stared at him. 'If her breathing is anything to go by then yes she had felt it too. I'll have to research this sensation between us. I wonder if it would happen again if I touch her? I don't think I'll get the chance again today though.'

Orenda was on her feet glaring at the two of them. Because Sarah still refused to look at the vampire in the eyes she couldn't see the woman's expression properly, but her mouth was set like she wasn't pleased with what had happened and her hands were clenched into fists.

'Hell, I'm not pleased about it.' The jaguar part of her was though.

While Itztecpatl thought, having noted the reaction of both women, 'Me and my jaguar spirit, however, are very pleased.'

Sarah picked up her walking stick then turned and ran for her life, which was more of a hobbling fast step at a sideways angle. Not pretty, but it allowed her to move faster than standard walking.

"Stop!" Orenda demanded.

Even though it hadn't been directed at him, he could feel the force behind the demand and it made him falter slightly. He saw her stop all of a sudden and almost lost her balance as she reached the door because of the tug the command had caused.

However, she forcibly reached her hand slowly out to grab the door knob, turn it and gradually forced herself out the door – because she couldn't go any faster against the compulsion, shut the door and left the premise.

Itztecpatl was surprised, pleased and proud of her strength. He never knew someone so small could be so strong of will against the mind force of a vampire. Naturally, he kept that all to himself as he didn't want to experience more of Orenda's temper than he was already expecting to receive.

"Leave me!" Orenda snapped.

He and Anoki left as quickly as was politely possible.

Sarah had to do it all slowly or she would have looked like a puppet on a string, extremely jerky movements. The further away she got from the Prince, the less grip the compulsion had on her. By the time she got home she was weak from the effort of fighting the compulsion and from relief. After making it inside, Sarah collapsed on the lounge and cried.

She cried in fear of what had happened and of what would happen next. In that moment, Sarah decided she was going to do her best to stay away from the Prince, but being her animal to call Sarah didn't hold out much hope.

'I don't think she will leave me alone so easily.'

Mick and Toby came into the lounge room at the sound of her crying.

"Sarah, what's wrong?" Mick asked. She could hear his concern without having to look at him.

Still she cried, she couldn't stop she was so afraid. Mick and

Toby could do nothing but comfort her until she could stop crying. However, when she did, she fell asleep.

When they tried to question her about it later, she realised she couldn't tell them. They were just human, even if they had worked for a vampire once. Sarah didn't want them involved with the Prince at all. Hell, she didn't want to be involved with the woman at all.

They weren't happy with her refusal to tell them but there was nothing much they could do about it.

An hour or so later, after other duties, once he and Anoki were alone...

"Well?" was all he asked.

"There haven't been any alpha females, let alone any strong enough for what's required of them, in years. The others aren't interested beyond bedding us and what status and privileges that gets them. She could be the one we have been waiting for." Anoki stated with quiet enthusiasm.

'Like the ruling classes throughout history, even we're a mixed group. Some want a pretty ornament, while others – such as myself – desire a strong partner to help us lead our clans.' Itztecpatl mused privately.

"My thoughts exactly. I need more information about her. Will you organise that for me please?"

"My pleasure." Anoki said with a smile.

Then Itztecpatl told him about the zapping attraction he and she had experienced and the two men discussed the implication. Not long after, Itztecpatl researched that electrical sensation.

Unfortunately, there was very little information about it but what he could find seemed to have something to do with the mating of two strong partners. However, because therians can't breed, it's believed to be a way to provide a strong leadership by joining a strong alpha male with an equally strong alpha female. Strength, however, didn't only refer to physical. It also referred to the strength of the spirit within.

Because it's so rare, there aren't enough chances to research and document it. 'Don't think I'm going to be offering either her or myself any time soon for it. However, what I've found out so far does seem to fit with my first meeting of her.'

After talking to those at the QTL, Itztecpatl and his trusted few had managed to find out her name only. It seemed those in the QTL seemed reluctant, maybe protective even, to talk about her.

'I find that piece of information interesting. Do they not know what she is capable of? That she's an alpha?' He frowned as he stared off into the distance. 'I just don't know enough.'

Chapter 11

It was the third week of January when Orenda had 'called' to Sarah again. She had fought it as best she could but... There she stood. She was also annoyed at her disappointment over no bare thighs and chest of one particular male the moment she saw him. 'He does look good in the jeans and grey t-shirt though.'

Orenda had more of her vampires and jaguars in the room with them that time round. Why? Itztecpatl didn't know. He hadn't been consulted. However, he thought the extra people weren't necessary but wasn't about to point it out to her; especially in front of everyone. For some reason he didn't have a very good feeling as to her reason/s for the larger audience. While he waited to see what would happen, he had a feeling he would have to confront Orenda over the situation.

'Something I'm not looking forward to.' He thought.

The moment Sarah stood in front of them, he could see she was still the little fire kitty he had first seen. She was angry and didn't seem to care who knew. This time she was dressed in jeans and a deep purple t-shirt and the same black open-toed slip-on shoes from last time. Even though she was dressed simply, to him she was very attractive.

"I can't believe you Orenda! I. Am. Not. Interested! Stop acting like a bitch in heat and get over it."

Itztecpatl couldn't believe his ears. The feistiness of her pleased him more and more. It took a lot of effort on his part to not grin at her words.

One of the Prince's vamps was suddenly in front of Sarah and hit her so hard and fast that she hadn't seen it or felt the fall. She certainly felt the impact of his hit on the side of her face though.

Itztecpatl was shocked and anger started to boil within him.

'She may not be officially one of my jaguars but it isn't his place to discipline her.' Unfortunately, there was nothing Itztecpatl could have done about it at that point in time. But time was on his side after all and he could wait until it was the right time.

Moving her tongue slightly, she tasted blood in her mouth and wiped the back of her hand gently against her mouth. It came away with more blood. Sarah rolled her eyes up at the offending vampire as she licked the blood from the back of her hand like a cat cleaning its paw. She let all see the anger she felt. However, her anger was also spurred by the lack of reaction and help from the Aztec and the other jags in the room.

Watching her, Itztecpatl's body reacted: blood and spirit beast singing. He noted the anger flash in her eyes as she looked up at the one who had struck her.

The vampire just sneered down at her in return, his contempt obvious.

Unfortunately, Sarah let her temper get the better of her. For the first time ever she changed at fight speed. It hurt but she was so pumped up on adrenalin, and the taste of blood, that she was unable to ignore it. What was left of her clothing slid and fell from her body as she slashed at the vampire who had hit her, decapitating him.

Itztecpatl only managed to follow her movements due to hanging around vampires for as long as he had.

"Order them to be still or they'll end up like him." Sarah growled, her tail flicking wildly showing her anger better than her therian face. The remnants of her clothing slid silently to the floor as she stood there.

His anger forgotten, Itztecpatl stared at her in stunned amazement.

'A white jaguar! She is a *white* jaguar!'

He had thought discovering she was an alpha had been the surprise but that paled compared to her colouring. He couldn't take his eyes off her. She was a gorgeous creamy white and, looking hard enough, he could see she had rosettes that were only a fraction darker in colour and shimmered a little more than the rest of her fur. She was stunning.

"You are a white jaguar?!" Orenda exclaimed as she motioned her people to stay still with a slicing of her hand. She was surprised and very excited about the revelation for some reason. A quick glance at the Prince's two main jaguars showed they too were excited.

"I could be purple with pink spots for all the good it would do you." She growled. Someone started to laugh but turned it into a cough. "Now, Back. The. Fuck. Off! Or you will regret it."

He stole a quick glance at Anoki. His friend briefly gazed at him and Itztecpatl saw the pleased glint in his friend's eyes as well.

Then he just stared at his little fire kitty. 'She is just so full of surprises. I so need time with her, and she is ours. Whether she knows it or not. Whether she likes it or not.' He had to keep a tight rein on himself so Orenda wouldn't pick up on his feelings. At least not yet.

"You owe me a life Sarah." Orenda stated calmly but Sarah could sense the woman's fury.

"No, I don't. You pushed and that was the price. You gambled and lost. You owe me clothing. No matter what anyone thinks I'm a lady and decent ladies don't go around naked. Makes me wonder, what sort of lady are you, Orenda?" Sarah knew anger was making her careless with her words and her voice extra growly. At that point she was beyond caring, she had had enough.

'Her anger makes her bold, but could get her into a lot of trouble.' He mused. 'Depending on Orenda's mood of course.' However, it didn't escape him the effect her voice had on his body as it tingled through him and he started to become aroused.

With something along the lines of annoyance, Orenda flicked her left wrist and Itztecpatl walked through a door behind him a little off to his left.

Sarah watched him turn on his heel and disappear through a door behind him. Then she resumed keeping an eye on everyone else in the room.

He entered a private chamber belonging to Orenda. Against

the far wall was a wardrobe. 'Sarah and Orenda are of similar builds, even if Orenda is taller and bigger in the breasts department, so her clothing should fit my little fire kitty without a problem.'

Opening the doors, he quickly rifled through the clothing within it and found a nice dark purple cotton dress that would come down to mid-calf on Sarah. 'Mind you, I wouldn't mind seeing her naked.' He thought with a slight smile.

Instead, he grabbed the dress off the hanger. 'At least I know she likes the colour.'

He walked back out to the audience room and watched her intently. He couldn't help but smile slightly as he strode towards her. 'She's a beautiful jaguar even if she doesn't look happy at the moment. I want to run my hands through her fur and capture her angrily flicking tail and caress and play with it till she calms down. Then play with it just for the fun of it.'

'Glad someone finds it all amusing. I know I don't.' Sarah thought sourly the moment she saw his expression.

He handed the dress to her. If she hadn't known any better Sarah would have said his fingers brushed hers deliberately just to have that sensation, along with their jaguars stirring, run through them. She tried to suppress the shiver but it was too intense, while he was able to suppress its effect upon him.

'Either that or it doesn't affect him at all.' She thought grumpily.

She wasn't happy about it. He, and everyone else who had been watching, noticed her reaction and it delighted him.

'It's just as strong for her as it is for me.' He couldn't hide his delight, and to be honest he didn't even try to hide it, but he gazed at her with a desire so strong it was becoming a need, a hunger for him.

'A hungry craving *only* for her.'

Reluctantly, but hiding it from Orenda and her court, he went back to his place beside Orenda and was surprised when Sarah hadn't asked them to turn around to give her privacy. Maybe she knew they wouldn't have done so. In retrospect, Itztecpatl guessed it wasn't very nice of them to not do so.

Sarah concentrated on getting dressed instead of him. She didn't bother asking them to turn around because she didn't think they would if she had asked. She did so instead – and thought how disappointed Kaelan would be with her for turning her back on them – and changed back to human, staggered slightly then dressed.

'And a lovely... *back*... she has too' Itztecpatl mused and thought about her nakedness under the dress. Only to close his eyes and struggled at reining in his thoughts and arousal. That much blood rushing south and it wouldn't be difficult for the vampires to notice. His jags wouldn't care.

Once facing them again, she realised no one had moved and all were watching her, especially Itztecpatl. There was a look on his face that she couldn't interpret. She frowned at him slightly.

Both he and his spirit wanted her and, by her frown when she glanced at him, he guessed his longing continued to show. He didn't care. The strength of his desire for her surprised him. Again, he didn't care.

"Thank you for not attacking me while my back was turned." She said softly, but still not pleased with the way things were going.

"Only cowards attack when the back is turned." Orenda responded.

Sarah nodded. "I'm leaving Orenda. I'm not interested. Please leave me alone." She turned and walked away. To her surprise, Orenda let her go without a fight or a word of any kind.

The first chance Anoki and Itztecpatl were alone…

"A white jaguar Itztecpatl! I can't believe it." Anoki exclaimed softly with excitement as he cornered his leader and friend.

Whether the average person understands it or not, humans aren't normally reclusive (despite the animals jaguars and leopards being so) and most therian's want to gather together, with their strain of therianthropy being the common factor. As a result, because they are human they tend to think like humans and therefore place a significance, an importance, on such rarities.

Itztecpatl grinned at him. "I know, I know."

"The real white jaguar is rare enough but I've never heard of a therian one before." Anoki stated with a slight frown.

"I know. Not only that but no one had ever mentioned the fact of her fur colour before. Definitely none of the leopards that's for certain and they would have known since she socialises with them during the full moon."

"What are you going to do?" His friend asked.

"I'll just have to try to get to know her personally. I want her part of our group." Itztecpatl stated intently. "In the meantime get someone to talk to Antonio about what happened to the one who created her. One white jaguar in Australia is amazing, but two is incredible. If the person is still in the country then we need to see if they will join us."

Over the following weeks, they learned that the one who created Sarah had been killed in the efforts of saving her life. There would be no other white jaguar to add to the group. 'Can't say I'm not disappointed but I'm glad Sarah had been saved.'

Over those same following weeks, Itztecpatl watched as Orenda tried to court Sarah with flowers and invites to the theatre, ballet and dinner; both public and in private. He was pleased to see Sarah had refused them all...

A couple of the prince's jaguars also tried to see Sarah. Not bothering to find out who they were, she refused them. After what she had been through with the Prince of the City, Sarah didn't want to know about any of them at any time in the immediate future, if ever. She also didn't want to see him due to his lack of help over the vampires' behaviour. Every time she thought about it, it left her furious.

She didn't understand that buzz that occurred both times they had touched. Not only that but she found him distractingly attractive.

'How can I be attracted to him if I love Kaelan?' She had no answer.

...However, Sarah also refused to see him.

For Itztecpatl, cornering her was all the more difficult because she barely left the property she lived on since she worked there as well. Besides, with humans living there as well as the vampires and therians who worked there, there was nothing he could do as he refused to break the law.

The one place she couldn't completely avoid him and other jags was at the therian meetings. Before that first audience with the Prince, she had never seen the Prince's two prime jaguars at the meetings since they had arrived in Brisbane. From that first audience they, and other jags, started attending the meetings. She suspected she was the reason for it.

For the first few meetings, they attended but only watched and listened to the proceedings and didn't go anywhere near Sarah. Then, one evening after the second audience with Orenda, he and the one with him walked towards her. The moment Sarah saw them bee-lining towards her she went still and her heart rate started beating harder. Then she turned to leave or at least disappear from their line of sight.

He watched her. Then it appeared she was trying to run away from him again. This time he wouldn't have it. With determination in his step, while keeping his eye on her retreating form, he politely made his way through the crowd to get to her.

Once she realised she wouldn't be able to avoid him, with quick glances around her and back at him, she found a deserted spot where she could warn him off without everyone else hearing them. As quickly as she could she headed over to it and turned around in time for him to be in touching distance.

Just as he was about to reach her...

Wide eyed she held up a warning finger and hissed quietly at him. "Stop right there and don't you dare touch me or you won't live long enough to regret it... or not. I want no public displays. I also prefer it if you left me alone!"

"So direct Sarah..." He started saying, an amused expression teasing his handsome features.

"I don't want any trouble or misunderstandings and I'm not in the mood for either." She interrupted as she attempted to ignore the effect of his voice on her body.

"...but you're being unreasonable..." He frowned slightly despite the small smile staying in place.

With his words, she was instantly angry. With a quick glance around the area, she checked her tone and hissed at him letting him see how not in the mood she was.

"Unreasonable?! *I'm* being unreasonable?! Stay away from me. Just you and yours stay the hell away from me."

As she started to back away she noted others at the meeting had turned to gaze curiously at them. It seemed her anger was radiating off her in palpable waves for others to sense. Glaring at him again, she shook her head and continued to move away.

"Sarah..." He called out in confusion and frustration.

"No." She stated simply and adamantly then turned and left.

With a frown, he sighed. On some level he couldn't blame her but he also couldn't help believing she was being unreasonable by not giving him a chance.

To her annoyance, it wouldn't be the last time he would try to talk to her. With the way Orenda ordered her around and they, he, had just stood there and allowed it she wasn't interested in making peace or talking to them. So much so, she enlisted the help of Antonio and Maria and the rest of her close friends to keep him and his away from her. Her friends seemed only too happy to help her after she explained why.

However, Itztecpatl noticed the closing of ranks and the cold shoulder the jags were starting to receive. While it surprised him, it also annoyed the hell out of him. He knew there was nothing he could do other than keep trying, if not as often as before. On a trivial note for him...

They were six months in their new country and it was hard to believe that much time had already passed. About a third to half of the coterie – Orenda, Max, Darius, Varrik, Anoki and Itztecpatl being some of them – had come to terms with the reversal of driving positions and the seasons, to name a couple, and were settling in quite nicely.

It helped that Brisbane was a lovely place to live. While most of them felt they could have done without the humidity, Itztecpatl for one, they were enjoying the place. He knew he would enjoy it more if things were better between him and her.

Receiving a break from the hassles of the Prince and her jags – as well as any other therian and vampiric politics, Sarah managed to find time for a spot of childish fun. Something that reminded her of when she was a child. The stereo was pumped up so she could hear it while lounging on the back verandah, hoping for a cool breeze. Mick was in the kitchen and Toby was somewhere else in the house.

Noting the clouds coming in, she stood up and went over to

the railing. She smiled. She could smell rain in the air. It would be a welcome relief from the heat and humidity. Heading down stairs, she noted the odd raindrop or two. Continuing over to the garage, she placed her walking stick against the garage door and waited.

"Sarah, what are you doing?" Toby called out as he stood at the railing on the verandah at the corner of the house as he watched her.

"Come and join me." She answered with a grin as she watched Mick stand beside him.

Then it started to rain lightly even though the sun was still shining. Steam wafting up from the hot cement driveway as the rain hit it; Sarah stretched out her arms and tilted her head back as she slowly turned 360 on the spot. The rain soaked into her dress, causing it to hug her body and cling to her legs. The guys just grinned at each other and made their way towards her. By the time they reached her, the rain was falling harder and all three were quickly drenched. In the distance they could hear the rumbles of thunder.

To top it off, Sarah heard the chorus to GANGgajang's *'Sounds of Then'*...

Out on the patio we'd sit,
And the humidity we'd breathe,
We'd watch the lightning crack over canefields
Laugh and think, this is Australia.

Sarah squeaked in surprise when Mick scooped her up and

turned on the spot faster than she was able to. With the three of them dancing around in the rain, Mick suddenly tossed her over to Toby. The three of them were laughing, enjoying themselves in the rain, with Sarah squealing every time Mick and Toby tossed her between them.

The radio then followed with Belinda Carlisle's *'Summer Rain'*...

Whispering our goodbyes
Waiting for a train
I was dancing with my baby
In the summer rain

The ten minutes of playing in the rain came to an end, after Toby caught her on the latest toss, when the rain stopped falling.

"I'll go get some towels." Mick offered with a breathless laugh. He dashed upstairs and disappeared.

Toby took her over to the stairs. Letting her slide down his body in setting her on her feet, her eyes widened in shock at the unexpected discovery. Him supporting her that way made it impossible to miss his state of arousal.

"Toby?!" She whispered wide eyed.

He stepped back and shook his head. Then he turned and retrieved her walking stick and, after handing it to her, started to head up stairs. She touched his forearm.

"We can't ignore this." She practically whispered.

"We can and we will." He stated quietly after a quick glance up at the verandah. Then he gently removed her hand and went up the stairs two at a time.

By the time she made it up stairs, Toby was nowhere in sight. By the time she finished having a shower and dressing, she found a note from him and the two men having gone out as planned.

Sarah,

This will be the only discussion on the subject. After you have read this there will be no mention of what happened at all.

There is nothing to discuss. What happened, happened. Just as you don't love me, I don't love you.

Let the matter drop here and now.

Toby.

Sarah stared at the note with mixed emotions. Relief he didn't love her swept through her, but was sure he was lying just to save her from dealing with the matter. She didn't know what to believe. His behaviour towards her since she had coloured her hair seemed to suggest he was lying. However, even she knew there have been times when friends have slept with each other but didn't commit to a relationship.

She sighed. She didn't know what to do so she decided to take his advice for the time being.

A few days later, Sarah opened her bedroom door but stopped herself from walking out when she overheard Mick and Toby talking in the lounge room.

"What's going on between you and Sarah?" Mick asked.

"What do you mean?" Toby sounded genuinely confused. She suspected he was acting but couldn't be sure.

"She's all quiet and seems to have retreated into herself."

"She has? Maybe... things are getting to her. You know what's she's like when things become too much for her. She's had it rough for the past few years. Maybe she's on the downside of that emotional roller coaster she's been strapped into..."

"Hmmm... Maybe..." Mick mused aloud.

"All we can do is give her space and time." Toby stated.

Leaning back against the wall out of sight, Sarah knew she had been acting shy and quiet around Toby but she couldn't help it. She took a deep breath then slowly let it out. She knew she would have to strive to act normal around them and knew it wasn't going to be easy. She waited another couple of minutes before heading to the kitchen like she originally intended.

~*~

Reading more of the reports however, Kaelan found it amusing to hear the new Prince of the City – who just so happened to be a woman – had the hots for her but Sarah kept refusing the Prince at every turn. 'Damn! But that has to irk the Prince big time.' That story had him chuckling for a while.

What didn't have him chuckling was the rumour of the

Prince having forced Sarah to the Prince's side but there's no confirmation about it and no one seemed willing to talk about it. Although, talk did get back to him about how the other therians had started to close ranks to protect Sarah from the Prince and her followers. That piece of information was very interesting.

Despite her being a therian, the other therians obviously saw her as an innocent. While it was good she was being protected, just how long would things stay that way? Weak therians didn't last long; not even in Brisbane. It was beside the point the Brisbane groups didn't hold with the old style hierarchy system any more; as there were always some who felt the weak didn't deserve to live at all.

'However, maybe I have underestimated her once again.'

Now the most interesting of those particular reports were the stories of two fights she had gotten herself into – while in the Prince's turf – and came out of without a scratch... The first one, she had apparently clawed the new Prince's head therian, who just so happens to be a jaguar as well. No real details other than she didn't kill him. The second one, it seemed she decapitated one of the Prince's blood suckers. Reason why, not revealed. Nor was how she had decapitated him revealed.

Hearing about those two reports almost had him regretting he hadn't been there to see it. However, he was surprised to hear she could fight like that and she was still alive. The reports have been adamant she hasn't been taking unarmed fighting lessons of any kind and he himself had never gotten around to teaching her any before she'd become therian. Once again she had him double guessing her capabilities and it frustrated the hell out of him.

'Maybe I do need to reacquaint myself with her again. Hmmm... something to think about indeed.'

A couple of days later, just over a year since he drove away, he had just finished an assignment when he logged into his laptop and checked what jobs were available. The moment he opened the program, a 'freshly listed' flag popped up. Kaelan clicked on it, read it and groaned with dread and disbelief. He claimed the hit before anyone else could then flopped back on the bed and stared at the ceiling while he waited for the details to come through.

'I had hoped this day would never come.'

Chapter 12

It was the last week of February and the end of summer, and Sarah couldn't believe another year had past again.

'I've been a therian for just over a year now and I've just celebrated my twenty-seventh birthday a couple of weeks ago. A nice present of not hearing from Orenda for these past few weeks though.'

No more 'calls' or invites or flowers. Maybe she had given up.

'Yeah right and it snows in hell too. She's up to something. I know it.' She thought cynically

It was a Saturday night, early evening, and the sun had just set. It was also days away from the full moon so Toby and Mick were out and about until after the full moon and she didn't have to work again until after the full moon.

Sarah was in the nail bar with a client for an emergency repair and fill because the woman had a function to attend. She had willingly paid the extra fee to have her nails done outside of normal business hours. Sarah was sitting at her table applying the last coat of polish to the client's nails when the door opened.

It was a little over a year ago when he had last left the place, and yeah he remembered it all too well. He couldn't forget no matter how hard he had tried.

'Because I've tried damned hard to do so.'

Gazing up at the house, he slowly entered the driveway; one of the few things which rarely changed in his life other than aging. He noted the lights on in the little building to the right of the house.

'Seems she's working. Rather unusual for her, to be working on a Saturday night. She usually doesn't any other time.' The reports had said she had stopped working evenings and weekends once she'd employed her staff. Slowly he drove up the left side of the house and parked sort of half way between the front and back of the house itself.

It wasn't a happy moment when he had left back then and it's not a happy moment to be back now. Turning the engine off, he leant his head against the steering wheel. He was not looking forward to it, but a promise was a promise and if nothing else he keeps his word.

Kaelan sighed, 'Might as well get it over with.' He got out of the Jeep and headed to the little building on the right side of the house. Opening the door and the old style doorbell chimed as he opened and closed it. Despite the additional tables and equipment, the place looked the same.

It was like walking into an English 1800's style shoppe and despite the mod cons, it looked awesome because the majority of them appeared like they were from the 1800s as well. Except for the EFTPOS machine, the uv lamps and some of the other equipment, no way to make them look like anything other than what they were. Other than that, everything else matched the theme.

He could see her with a client and even though he didn't know much about the business it seemed like she was almost finished. At first he thought it wasn't her, she had red hair, but then she lifted her face up a little and he could see it was definitely her.

'Damn! She looks so stunning as a red head, and I mean a red head. Not orange or any other claims of red.' His chest tightened as he gazed at her.

She didn't make eye contact when she said, "Have a seat. I'll be with you shortly." Even though her voice was pleasant, Sarah was not impressed that there was another client when it was her time off. She had been hoping for an early night.

'No such luck now it seems.' It took a lot of effort to stay pleasant.

She placed the client's hands in a dish of icy cold water, for a few minutes – to help them dry faster. A tip she used during warmer weather only. Then she instructed the client to be careful with the polish and not to knock the nails too hard for a day or two. After removing the woman's hands from the water, Sarah set them in front of a fan to help dry the water off her hands. By not drying her hands with a towel it reduced the risks of smudging the paint job.

Thankfully, Sarah had the client pay for the service before applying the polish. Nothing worse than doing a wonderful paint job only for the client to smudge them in some way while getting cash or a credit card out. She preferred using gel polishes but still had some clients who persisted in wanted standard nail polish. At least with gel polishes they were smudge-less the moment the nails came out of the uv lamp.

"There you go Mrs Hardings, all done. You have your appointment for two weeks' time already so I'll see you then. Now be careful of your nails."

"Thank you so much Dear and I will. You *are* a lifesaver. See you in two weeks." Mrs Hardings said in that exaggerated chirpy and hyper tone of hers.

'Now, that woman would get on my nerves really quickly.' Kaelan reflected. She was a woman in her fifties and definitely showing her age but dressed in a form fitting black sleeveless number which came just above her knees.

'Would be okay I guess if her body suited the dress; but it doesn't.' She also had a slightly high pitched nasally voice with what sounded, to him, like a faked breathiness. To him, she looked like an overdressed hyena.

'I wonder if I could get away with killing her as a form of therapy' He mentally sighed as he knew it was just wishful thinking on his part, knowing he would never go through with it. 'But how I wish.'

Sarah stood up to escort the woman to the door when she finally saw who was sitting in the waiting area. She paused slightly, eyes widening in surprise and a slight smile started at her lips, then continued to the door with Mrs Hardings. She also couldn't help noticing how Mrs Hardings didn't take her eyes off him as she headed to the door. Or how Mrs Hardings almost walked into the door.

Sarah had to bite the inside of her lip to stop herself from laughing out loud. However, it pleased her to note that he never glanced at her client the moment Sarah had spotted him in the waiting area. Once again Sarah discovered the butterflies were alive and well the moment she saw him.

Drinking the sight of her in, she was dressed in an ankle length navy blue pleated skirt and an untucked long sleeved sky blue polo shirt with her business name embroidered in navy blue on the left breast pocket. She also wore either navy blue or black court shoes but no pantyhose or the like. Her clothing just made her hair colour stand out all the more.

He noticed her pause as her eyes widened with surprise. Barely a moment later a smile started to show and it made him feel worse for being there. Then she was all business again as she continued to the door, escorting the client out while repeating cautions and appointment time and finally saying good bye. Then she flipped the sign from Open to Closed and turned towards him.

She couldn't hide her smile when she greeted softly, "Kaelan, wonderful to see you. You in town for business or pleasure?"

He wasn't smiling. It wasn't a good sign and she was dreading what he would say.

'She just had to ask it that way didn't she?' As a result he couldn't avoid answering truthfully or delay telling her the reason.

"Hello Sarah. Business." He said neutrally. He couldn't return her smile because he knew his comment would wipe hers away.

Her smile died. She thought she died a little inside as well.

"When?" While she had suspected it would happen, Sarah had hoped it never would and while she hoped she was wrong as to his reason for being back, she didn't think she was.

Just like that, she instantly knew why he was there. 'Still the perceptive bunny.'

"Four days from now."

Sarah just nodded. Four days. She turned away from him. She should have known it would have been the only reason for him to be anywhere near her again. It was too much to hope it would have been for some other reason.

"You're looking good. Red suits you." He commented quietly, just to change the subject temporarily. She didn't look happy at his comment though, 'not that I blame her I guess.'

'Oh yeah, he hadn't seen my new hair and clothes yet. Not that it matters now.'

"And then I'll be dead." She responded blandly. "Between now and then can you please try to find out who placed the hit please? I want to ask them why."

"Okay, I'll try to find out for you." 'I'm guessing she'll also try to get them to call it off. If there's even a small chance she can then why not find out for her.'

"Thank you. On the final day, do it at the paintball range where we first met. Seems fitting somehow."

'Yes, very fitting, full circle even. I've just been told that I have four days left to live but my voice is still bland as I discuss plans for my impending death. What is the matter with me?' She couldn't seem to get worked up about it. Not right then.

He was surprised she had a location picked out and that

particular one of all places. 'Fitting? I don't know if I would say it was fitting but it's definitely ironic. The place which started my curiosity about her abilities to begin with.' With a mental sigh, he knew he would agree.

"You're taking this better than I thought you would. Better than a lot of others would and have." He said cautiously. He hadn't missed the lack of emotion in her voice and was worried she was giving up. Strangely, that thought irritated him as well.

She turned around and stared at him, but not with anger or despair like he had been expecting. "What would it accomplish to react any other way Kaelan? Should I rant and rage, cry and throw things? Would any of that change the outcome?" Her voice faded to a stop. The tears were welling but they hadn't spilled. Turning around she walk a few steps away from him.

"For what it's worth Sarah, I'm sorry." and he sounded it.

"Why? I'm the one who asked you to do this should it happen." She responded softly with her back to him.

"I'm sorry I let my desire to see you in action caused you to become a therian..." They were just words but he had to say them because he truly did mean them.

However, thrown completely off guard, she surprised him. 'She moves better now than she had the last time I saw her.'

She didn't let him finish. Half way through his apology Sarah stormed towards him and thumped him in the chest just like a clichéd girl, but without using her therian strength which also surprised him. Then again, and again and again and the tears flowed as he held her, her hands against his chest, trapped between their bodies.

"It's not your fault. It's not your fault." She cried over and over softly, her voice muffled against his chest. All the while he was steady, like a rock as always, as he just held her. Perversely, she found it comforting.

While he could do nothing but hold her and let her get it out of her system, or part of it at least.

After a few moments she calmed down enough to gently push away from him and he let her. Now that she had calmed down she was embarrassed at being against him like that, but it felt so good. "You're welcome to stay if you want. It's still your house after all." She said softly.

"People don't normally invite their killers to stay Sarah." He sounded surprised. When he least expected it she surprised the hell out of him and he couldn't keep it from his voice. With that invite, he knew she hadn't really changed. Still so accepting.

"And I told you before I'm not normal people. Besides, you're doing this because I made you promise remember." Her voice was barely above a whisper but it was so quiet in the room that she knew he could hear her.

Therian or not she truly hadn't changed at all. Once again she was back to not looking at him.

"Yeah, I remember." But he didn't exactly sound happy about it. Sort of. While he wasn't happy about having to fulfil the promise, a small, or not so small, part of him was looking forward to coming up against her. He mentally shook himself because it was that attitude that caused her to become what she was now in the first place.

"Your choice, the offer is there. I still have work to do here before I can go home." She turned away from him. It was a few moments before she heard the door open and close.

With a sigh, she set about cleaning the nail bar, setting up for after the full moon and taking the rubbish out on her way out the door. She had given all staff time off as a little holiday time. Now that Kaelan was back in town, looked like it had been a good decision.

Just like that, she had dismissed him. While he couldn't blame her for treating him in such a way, it still irked him that she had. He stood there for a moment, wanting to go mad at her and wanting her to look at him, something. Anything. Instead, he walked out and saw her start cleaning the place.

Once inside the house, he took a shower but didn't linger. Trying to find his toiletries had taken long enough; even if he had been pleased to see her feminine gear hadn't overrun the bathroom. He was pleased to see the layout of the bedroom hadn't changed; only with the exception of his mother's dressing table and matching chair had been added. It also pleased him to see it neat and tidy and not overflowing with personal products women seemed to accumulate.

After finishing, he went to the tallboy to find fresh clothing to wear only to be confronted with her things. 'Pretty things, pretty little lacy things, but where the hell are mine?'

Opening drawer after drawer and all he could find were her clothing until reaching the second last drawer. He looked in the bottom drawer as well and found more of his clothing. 'Typical bloody woman! Waltzes in and, left alone for a bit, rearranges everything without warning a man.'

Grabbing what was needed he went to the wardrobe and

found the same situation. Some very lovely clothing – with more lace amongst other fabrics – with his shoved to the far left and on the top shelf. Shaking his head and taking what he wanted and threw them on the bed with the first lot he had grabbed. 'After dressing I might browse through her clothing. Having chosen her clothing during those first three months, I've never seen what she likes to wear. I never thought to take her shopping during that time. While the fabrics look great it doesn't mean her choice in styles are.'

Throwing the towel at the foot of the bed he started pulling his briefs on. They'd just reached mid-thigh when he heard the bedroom door open, a soft intake of breath then the door closing before he could turn around.

She didn't see Kaelan's car out the front as she walked up the front stairs of the house. It seemed like he had chosen not to stay and she was disappointed despite the reason he was back. For once she was successful in fighting off the tears which had threatened to spill. Finally, she dumped the keys on the little display table beside the front door.

After closing the front door, she walked down the hallway into the lounge room and kicked her shoes off so they were with the rest of them, then started stripping out of her uniform until she was down to underwear.

With her clothes over her left arm and leaning heavily on the walking stick, she headed back up the hallway to the bedroom so she could have a shower and find something comfy to wear. All of a sudden she was tired. 'If I didn't have to do dinner I would crash here and now but I do have to eat.'

Sarah opened the bedroom door and caught a view of a bare back covered in scars and a naked rear end before a pair of boxer briefs could be pulled over that firm shapely bare butt. She turned as fast as she could and shut the door then slumped against it.

'Far out space cookies! He's staying. Niiiice butt!' She thought and sighed, fanning herself from the heated blush that swept over her face. 'I don't care if I die tonight, that was a sight worth having him back for.'

A few seconds of trying to recover, she was about to move away from the door when it opened and she started to fall backwards. She let out one of those little girly squeals in fright then he caught her. She gazed up at him from bare chest to face – she couldn't see lower, and he looked down at her, then down the length of her and her state of undress. He did have the better view point. There was a look in his eyes and she couldn't read it. She didn't understand why, but she couldn't.

He couldn't help the leisurely gaze down the length of her mostly naked body. Nice shimmery dark blue lace underwear with pale flesh peeking through was all that came to his mind. He didn't have enough right of mind to school his expression to neutral. Not with her looking like that and in his arms.

The blush that had been receding came back in full force. "You know you're still too tall." She whispered then mentally groaned at the stupid thing to say. It was all so déjà vu-ish.

"And you know you are still too short." His voice was lower than he intended as blood rushed south. He was suddenly hit with an instance of déjà vu. Different reasons but almost the exact same words as just over a year ago. While she blushed, the blood for him rushed south and his pants suddenly became too tight.

'She hasn't changed at all. Her skin is still creamy pale and oh so soft against my hands.'

After he set her back on her feet, he thought it was amusing when she brought her left arm up over her breasts so her clothing covered her. He was pleased to see she still had her rainbow bee eater tattoo. He opened the bedroom door wider and stepped aside so she could enter. He couldn't take his eyes away from her. He didn't want to take his eyes away from her.

Sarah blushed harder as Kaelan gently set her upright. She knew he had seen her in less but she couldn't help bringing her left arm with the clothing on it across her chest. Opening the door wider, he stepped aside so she could go through. Then she noted, with more than a little disappointment, that he had managed to get on a pair of jeans before rushing out. She did note the zip was only half way up and the button still undone.

'God! What a sexy sight!' Then she dragged her thoughts away from that particular territory. However, it did remind her of something else.

"Oh, I guess I should have told you that I have moved your clothing about so it was easier for me to reach my things. Socks, joxs and t-shirts are in the second last drawer, track pants and some polo shirts are in the bottom drawer of the tallboy, with the rest being in the wardrobe. The hanging clothes are on the far left with everything else on the entire top shelf." She informed softly, blushing profusely.

"Ah that's where everything is." He said sounding slightly amused. 'Hmm, the rearranging now makes sense. No, despite being a therian she hasn't changed at all. Still the tiny shy baby bunny.'

In that moment she got the impression he had already found them. She just nodded and hobbled past him. She went to the wardrobe...

The bedroom door closed, with him not in the room.

...to grab a light dress to slip on.

He watched at her for a moment. Her hair was longer than when he had last seen her... 'Just above her cute shapely bottom now.' ...and she had lost the rest of her excess weight. He guessed being therian was the cause for the rest of her new figure. Despite her weight back then he truly had thought she was cute, but now she was amazing as he stared at her for a few moments longer. As she went to the wardrobe, he grabbed the rest of his clothing, left the room and closed the door behind him.

Sighing, he then entered the spare bedroom since it looked like that would be where he would be staying. He set up his laptop and started one of the money tracer programs then set the volume up a little louder than usual so he could hear it in any part of the house. 'If she can't stop the person then they'll be my next hit. Free of charge. Hell! I might do them regardless and take immense joy in doing so I think.'

Forgoing the shower and entering the kitchen – he wasn't there – to make a cuppa and something to eat. Sarah decided on something simple since she had chicken out already. She sliced it into strips, seasoned it with herbs, spices and lemon juice and fried them in a little amount of macadamia oil. Then she cooked up some rice with coconut cream and a little more herbs and spices.

Because Kaelan had decided to stay she automatically made enough for him as well. However, she was making enough noise around herself that she didn't hear him enter. Normally she didn't make that much noise but she did so just then in the effort to stop her mind from thinking too hard about the sight of him earlier.

After a few minutes he heard her go out into the kitchen. Once he had finished setting everything up and finished dressing, he decided to join her. Standing next to the work island, he watched her as she prepared some chicken, fresh vegetables and started cooking some rice. 'Never seen her cook before. I'd always organised the food.'

However, while not making that much noise, she was still noisy enough she hadn't heard him come in the room. Glancing briefly out the window he could see the vague outline of the bushland and a deer that had wandered close to the tree line and he was reminded about some information he had received last year and was suddenly so disappointed with her. Jealousy also raised its ugly head again and the whole situation, then and now, just made him so angry.

When she turned around, Sarah jumped in fright with him being so close. "Make some noise for goodness sakes, or is this your method of trying to kill me?" She gasped at him, her heart pounding so hard. She closed her eyes and took in deep slow breaths.

"Sorry, I forgot how jumpy you get." He didn't look sorry, he was smiling too much. However, it didn't seem to be his normal smile but she couldn't work out what was wrong with it.

"Yeah right." She grumped at him.

Funny how she didn't believe him. "So, how have your full moon parties been?" he asked pleasantly. In fact, too pleasantly.

"Oh I see you've kept tabs on what happens here." She shook her head. 'I should have known.' Sarah moved around the island so she was slightly less than arm's length away from him.

"I've always had the local watchers inform me as to what's happening around Brisbane and my home. They said you've had the same five people around for a while at the beginning. Who was the skinny naked therian you were always with?"

To her, his tone didn't sound so friendly any more. 'So that's the burr. Not that I understand why.' She thought as annoyance started to brew inside her.

He watched her intently and it was only because he had underestimated her yet again he had let what had happened next happen.

Without thinking, and because he was so close, she lashed out at him in anger and hit him with the flat of her hand in the centre of his chest and set him, hard, on his delectable rear end. A small part of her was satisfied at seeing him wince in pain when he hit the floor so hard.

Not only did he not get the chance to react but he also didn't get the chance to blink when she suddenly hit him hard with the flat of her hand and he started falling. Kaelan did two things... One: thought the shove really hurt, that he was going to have a bruise and two: pulled his gun from the small of his back. Because he was reaching for his gun and aiming as he fell that he didn't have his hands free to ease his hitting the floor. As a result he landed hard and couldn't stop from wincing when he impacted with the floor.

However, he had the gun aimed at her just before he landed. And a good thing too, because for the first time, Kaelan saw her truly angry and her anger was directed at him.

With her hands clenched into fists, "If your informants were really good enough they would have told you that nothing happened between us. I was always dressed and I no longer have him around anymore because he was becoming attached to me but not me to him. Now, I promise you this Kaelan Ridgeleigh, I will never attack you to kill you before the night of the full moon. You're safe from me so you can put your bloody gun away, but don't you *ever* treat me like that again. I'm not like that, never have been and never will be."

She was so mad and she let it show. Despite what she had just said, he hadn't put his gun away, so she turned her back on him and resumed tending to dinner. She had to, so she could hide the tears gathering in her eyes because his words and actions had hurt so much. Sarah practiced breathing even and barely blinking until the tears went away without spilling.

He kept his gun pointed at her as he kept his face neutral and just stared at her. Then she had the audacity to turn her back on him. He couldn't believe it. She just kept going with dinner. 'What's happening?! Why doesn't she attack?! She's angry enough to do so. Blasted inconsistent women!'

He stood up and put the gun away as she started to serve dinner. He stared at her as neutrally as possible. 'Maybe she isn't attacking because she plans on poisoning me.'

As she started to serve, he was finally standing up, gun away – probably tucked behind his back in his pants - and regarded

183

her not so nicely. At that point in time she didn't care. "Well, grab cutlery so we can eat." She said in exasperation and headed to the table with their plates.

He just stared at her. 'Is that what she's planning? To poison me?' While he felt silly for thinking it, it could still have been a possibility since he didn't really know her that well.

She glared at him with a frown when he hadn't moved. "What? What's wrong now?"

He shook his head and grabbed the cutlery. Then they ate.

He paused momentarily until she took her first mouthful then he had some of his. While he was surprised and pleased she wasn't attempting to poison him, he was very surprised she was able to cook so well.

"This is good." He sounded astonished. However, she hadn't missed the point of him taking his first mouthful after she had started eating.

"Thank you." She said quietly. She suspected he thought she was going to poison him and that idea upset her because she would never do such a thing. Again, she had to fight the tears and kept her head down for the duration. The pair ate in silence and without any eye contact from her at all.

When they finished, Sarah collected the dishes and started to wash them. After she poured a small amount of detergent into the sink – the bottle with the type of squirt lid that one pulls up to open and press down to close – she had the lid mostly but not quite closed. Then she did what she always did when doing the dishes...

Kaelan had to admit he was curious as to why she was just

standing there doing nothing.

...She waited a second or two with the bottle in her hand then gave it a practiced squeeze that sent bubbles flying up into the air, only for them to start floating down around her. She waited a couple more seconds then squeezed the bottle again shooting more bubbles up into the air. She repeated the action three more times, watching the bubbles floating around her. She was smiling at the bubbles as she gently blew them away from her mouth.

'I can't help it. I just love them immensely, listening to them pop as they hit my hair.' She thought to herself.

It was like watching a child, her face was so innocent looking in the simple joy of watching the bubbles around her. She squeezed the bottle a few more times and the area around the sink was full of tiny bubbles. Bubbles were on her hair, shoulders and clothing. Occasionally she would blow them gently away from her as they neared her lips. He couldn't help it but he laughed at her antics. She looked so delightful. He just couldn't imagine why anyone would want to kill her. 'Throttle her maybe, but kill her?'

Sarah had sort of forgotten that Kaelan was still in the room until he laughed at her. She blushed and did the dishes while he dried, grinning at her. Once she had finished she turned to him.

"You can sleep in the master bedroom and I'll sleep in the other room." She informed softly.

"No, you stay in the master bedroom and I'll sleep in the other room." He couldn't displace her from the room since she had been sleeping there for the past year.

"Damn it Kaelan. The house is yours and I'm not going to

sleep in your bed while you're here so you may as well sleep in it." She said quietly in a very tired voice then walked out on to the back verandah staring out at nothing.

An evening that was supposed to be a pleasant time just kept getting worse and worse. She didn't understand why they were at logger-heads with each other, why it seemed like they had to argue about everything. All she ever wanted was the time to go smoothly between them, but it never seemed to.

'What the hell just happened? I was being the gentleman and she just goes off at me?' He walked up behind her.

"What's wrong Sarah?" He asked.

It sounded like he was right behind her. She never heard him unless he wanted her to. Even with her enhanced hearing. With her back to him, she opened her mouth to say something, anything but nothing came out so she closed her mouth and shook her head instead.

It seemed to him that she refused to look at him and answer him. 'ARGH! What is it with this woman?!' He clenched his fists.

"Damn it! You are the most frustrating person I have ever met." And just like that she had him angry at her yet again.

She still didn't respond so he turned around and stormed off or he would have throttled her if he had stayed. He got into the Jeep and drove away with the need to try to calm down.

Chapter 13

No longer hearing the Jeep, Sarah sighed and went back inside. Even though she was tired, she couldn't sleep so she decided to do something, anything. She tried to relax with a book in the sitting room but it didn't keep her mind from thinking about him. So, after about ten minutes of trying to read the same page, she put the book down and went into the lounge room instead.

Then she sat at the keyboard and played. She started off with Mark Knopfler's *'Going Home'* – a lovely instrumental piece, then moved onto something else so she could play and change the way it sounded. She just played the piece over and over, making changes with each round. Basically something she always did when on the keyboard.

Sarah didn't know how long she spent playing it as she got herself lost in the music, or tried to. To her, it pretty much sounded the way she felt, sad and angry. Sad because Kaelan and she would never be together now and angry because she kept stuffing up their time together. She had done that over a year ago when he had saved her life. She couldn't seem to do anything right where he was concerned. She didn't understand why but that was the way it always seemed to happen between them.

However, she kept playing and kept tweaking the piece to the way she wanted it to sound. Eventually she paused because she was so damned tired and the music wasn't really helping any. She stared at the keyboard with her hands sitting limply in her lap.

Kaelan didn't get far before realising he was taking his frustrations out on her because he didn't really want to do the hit. Eventually, he realised he was trying to make himself feel better about it by antagonising her into attacking him so he could shoot her with a clear conscience. Only, he had just discovered she had better restraint than he thought she would have.

'I guess I should have known she would.'

Realising all that in barely thirteen minutes of driving like a hoon around the suburban streets of his neighbourhood, he sighed and headed back home. He had to apologise to her.

Getting out of the car, he could hear music playing. Quietly climbing up the stairs, he entered the house, via the back door, and went into the lounge room. He paused at the entryway. She was sitting at the keyboard he had left amongst her stuff and was playing a piece he vaguely recognised. Then she paused and he was about to say something when she started playing the piece again.

He listened but started noticing changes. She was changing bits of it as she played. He didn't know why but yet again she had surprised him with her capabilities and talents. He just stood there and listened to her play the piece over and over and change sections of it each time. Parts of it sounded sad while other elements sounded almost energetic or angry-like.

The last time she played the piece it sounded like the one before it as if she was satisfied with the way it sounded. Then she placed her hands in her lap and just stared at the keyboard.

"You're good. I didn't realise you played so well."

Sarah let out a little scream of fright and almost fell off the seat at the sound of Kaelan's quiet and gentle voice.

'Damn it but I tried not to scare her.'

With her heart pounding away in fright, she then bit her tongue real hard so she wouldn't snap at him, but damn, it was hard not to. She lifted a shaking hand to brush her hair out of her face, but clenched it into a fist to try to stop the shaking.

"Sarah, I'm sorry. I didn't mean to scare you." He said sounding apologetic as he came towards her. Her lips were pressed tight as if she was trying not to go mad at him. He wouldn't have blamed her if she had; he hadn't exactly nice to her earlier.

She could see the concern in his eyes as he frowned. He appeared worried as if she would bite his head off or something similar. She was still biting her tongue so she had to unclench her jaw before she could say something. She tasted blood, letting her know she had bitten too hard. "I didn't hear you come back."

'There, that was diplomatic even if it was said with a shaking voice.' She admitted privately to herself.

"How long have you been there?" She sat there as she tried

to calm her pounding heart.

Since she was trying to be nice he decided to try as well. "A while. It's been two hours since I first drove away, but I've been here long enough to listen to you change sections of the piece a number of times."

She nodded then murmured. "Thank you for the keyboard by the way."

"What makes you think I gave it to you?" His voice went neutral. He couldn't help it. He hadn't told anyone he had placed it amongst her stuff.

"I found the note paper I had written the list on and saw the words 'now have' beside the keyboard. The writing was yours."

"How do you know what my writing looks like?" He frowned at her. 'She knew my writing?'

Sarah gave him a 'get real' type of look. "Oh come on now, Kaelan. We've lived under the one roof for just over three months and I watched you write things down, watched you write out my exercise regime. When I looked at it I could see your writing. In this household, it was instantly recognisable to me. Didn't have to be Sherlock to work it out when I saw the same writing on my piece of paper."

'Heh, I'd forgotten she could be observant.' He smiled at her comment. "You're welcome. I'm glad you're enjoying it."

"I am." She smiled tiredly. The scare left her feeling totally exhausted.

A solution to their dilemma suddenly popped into his mind and he had no idea as to why it hadn't occur to him earlier.

"Tell you what. I'll sleep in *my* bed if you will as well, since it's been your bed for the past year. Besides, it's big enough for the two of us with plenty of room to spare." He gazed at her with a very serious look, while wearing a slight smile. He gave her his 'won't take no for an answer' look.

Sarah's eyes widened slightly. "Okay." She whispered after a small pause. 'I can't believe he's making such an offer. This will be the only chance I'll get so no way am I going to turn it down.'

Just like that, there was that scared baby bunny look and he had been expecting her to object some more. He was surprised when she hadn't.

"Good. You look beat." He said gently as he held his arm out to her. He was thrilled she'd agreed; let alone without argument.

Timidly, Sarah placed her hand on his arm and grabbed her walking stick and he slowed his pace to match hers as he escorted her to the bedroom. She didn't know why she was so shy; it wasn't like anything was going to happen. She then leant her stick between the bed and the bedside table, collected what she would wear to bed and went into the bathroom. He hadn't quite seen what it was she had grabbed from under her pillow.

She was about to put them on when she looked at them, then shrugged as he had seen her in them before; boxer briefs and tank top. Before he saved her she used to wear a nightie, but for some reason she hadn't gone back to wearing them. Maybe she would, but that was a thought for another time.

While she was in there, he stripped and put his pyjama pants on and got into bed on the other side from where he used to sleep. He didn't know whether to be annoyed or amused over having been displaced from areas that had been his since his late teens.

He also noted a weird looking extremely long looking pillow on her side of the bed. At first he thought it was one of those body pillows women drape themselves over but it wasn't shaped like a typical pillow. Hearing the en suite door, he ignored it for the time being.

Lying on his side, head on his hand propping him up, he watched her as she came out of the bathroom. She was wearing boxer briefs and tank top like the last time he saw her but looking way sexier now. Then he mentally groaned. 'God! I needed cold showers back then. I can see the hot water bill is not going to rise while I'm here.'

As she went to the dressing table, she couldn't help noticing he was shirtless. Sitting down, she applied some moisturiser to her hands and face until it had vanished into her skin. He didn't take his eyes from her at all.

'Thank goodness it isn't the mask type to be layered on and looked green. Would have hated waking up to that particular sight.' He mused critically to himself.

She then brushed her hair and he just watched her move. Even though he knew she still looked soft and tender he could see, as she brushed her hair, the hint of muscles moving. She noticed him watching her when she looked at him via the mirror and their eyes met briefly. She blushed, glanced down and continued brushing her hair.

'My insides always flip and flutter whenever he looks at me, watches me and I find it impossible not to blush when I see him doing so.'

'I don't think I've ever met a woman who blushes as much as

she does.'

Sarah continued to brush her hair until it crackled and strands started to float from the static electricity. She slowly put the brush down after cleaning it then climbed into bed. Draping herself over the body pillow, she rolled onto her side with her back to him and he could see her white panther tattoo. He was so tempted to touch it, to trace it with his finger. She reached out with her left hand, which took her panther slightly out of easy reach, and turned her lamp off.

"Good night Kaelan." She said softly. Yes she was tired but she was so nervous.

Trying to ease her nervousness he rolled onto his side so his back was to her, "Night Sarah." He responded just as quietly.

She tried to relax but she couldn't sleep. She tried to see if she could get a little more comfortable but to no avail. It took her a little while, but she was as comfortable as she was going to get. Eventually, though, she did manage to fall asleep. By that stage his eyes were accustomed to the darkness and he noted the soft glow of the nightlight he had plugged in for her when he had first brought her to his house. With a slight smile, he then let himself fall asleep as well.

Chapter 14

Kaelan woke up before the sun started shining into the bedroom. When the sunlight did begin to shine through the window, he had to close his eyes. He was about to roll away from the bright sunlight when he remembered she was beside him.

Feeling her warmth behind him, he just laid there and enjoyed it. He had actually dreamt of a moment like that, to wake up beside her. The way it was right then would more than likely be the closest he would get to something like it. Then he heard her breathing change.

The sun was streaming in by the time she awoke. Sarah moved slightly only to feel the rear end of someone lightly touching hers. She stilled and, at first, she couldn't work out why there would be another person in her bed then she remembered. She rolled over to confirm it and he rolled over towards her at the same time. She didn't know what sort of expression was on her face but he suddenly appeared amused.

He was greeted with the scared baby bunny look. As far as he was concerned, in that moment, it was a wonderful sight first thing in the morning. He smiled at her.

"Morning." She croaked then cleared her throat.

"Morning Sarah." He couldn't keep the amusement out of his voice.

He watched her as she lay on her back and stretched. He caught a glimpse of her rainbow bee eater tattoo on the inner side of her right breast and he had to resist the urge to pet it.

Despite him sounding amused with her, she liked the way he says her name, almost in a breathy manner. Not harsh and clipped like most say it. Even when he's angry at her he still says her name as if he's breathing it out. She resettled herself onto her back and stretched.

"You can have the bathroom first if you want. I want to sit here for a bit so I don't have to use my walking stick straight away." She offered shyly.

"Okay, thanks." He sat up and started to stretch when he suddenly felt her touch one of the knife scars round the middle of his back

When he had started to stretch, she got a good view of the scars on his back and some of the ones on his arms. She could only guess at what made them but some appeared to be burns, blade and bullet. If anything else then she didn't have a clue. She knew none of them were claw or teeth marks or he would have been therian. And he definitely wasn't that.

Without thinking it through, she reached out and gently, barely, daringly, touched one in the middle of his back. She was afraid to do more than that light touch for fear of how he would react. The one she touched was a long thin one as if it was made by a blade or the like.

To him, it felt very light – almost feathery. He couldn't help it but he went still. Her touch was almost electric as the spot tingled with her slight movements that caused his breath to catch in his throat.

"So many. Any so bad that they nearly took your life?" She whispered.

Kaelan closed his eyes. Her innocent touch, how he wanted it to be more than just innocent. Then he mentally shook himself. 'I can't, I can't do this!'

"No." He said almost abruptly then stood up and started to head for the bathroom, round the other side of the bed.

She let her hand fall. 'His reaction was better than I had been expecting I guess.'

She swung her legs over the edge of the bed to sit on the side. Her hands gripped the edge of the mattress and she just stared at the floor as he walked around the bed and passed her as he went into the bathroom. She let her mind go blank because she was embarrassed enough as it was. To her, it was just a too intimate a moment and she couldn't believe she had done that.

He almost paused to tell her it was okay but he didn't because none of it was. He went had his shower. He turned the water on a little colder than he liked it but, leaning forward with his arms stretched out in front of him and his hands pressed against the tiled wall, he just stood under it as his heart pounded.

'It's such shitty timing! All of it! The hit, these little things I feel for her. The little things she does that makes her so damned cute, her tenderness. I don't understand why someone wants her dead. For the amount of money offered it sounds too personal. Yet, there doesn't seem to be a lover. Spurned or otherwise. My watchers have confirmed that fact. Oh I knew she and that skinny therian weren't together. That was just me being a bastard to her last night, in the hope she would attack me so I could feel justified in killing her. But why? Why does someone want her dead?'

With no answers he finished his shower and walked out of the bathroom with a towel wrapped around him and she practically fled into the bathroom. He let her as he watched her. There was nothing he could do to soothe her in any way.

He grabbed himself one of the newer pairs of jeans to wear. While he was at the wardrobe, he perused through her clothing. Some interesting choices she had there. He chose a multi coloured blue skirt with layers of velvet and lace and plenty of ruffles. He also chose what looked like a blue brocade corset with darker blue lace sleeves that had scalloped cuffs.

The corset had silver hook and eyes at the front and silver cord as the lacing for the back. He fingered the soft lush fabrics, 'Very nice and very interesting.' He laid them on the bed then walked out, hoping she would wear them. He didn't know why it mattered to him, but it did.

'What? Haven't you met a guy who isn't a fashion designer who's interested in what a woman wears and actually knows what the fabrics are? Believe it or not, whether rare or not, we do exist.' He reflected to himself then shook his head at his silly musings.

While he waited for her, he made breakfast. However, in doing so, he noted three new cookbooks. Picking up the first one, he was about to flick through it when the intro page caught his attention. He quickly read the first couple of paragraphs and was surprised.

'Who would have thought the beasts educating themselves and each other on how to eat properly and to control their beasts?' Then he frowned at himself. 'I guess I shouldn't think that way since she certainly hasn't changed despite becoming one of them.'

Once he heard the shower stop, he put the book back then made her a cup of tea. He decided to go through those cookbooks later. After setting their breakfast on the table, he sat in his usual spot and waited for her. By the time he had finished his coffee, she finally came out with her head down.

After a while, Kaelan came out with a towel wrapped low around his hips; he looked awesome and fit, and fit for... Not finishing that thought, she fled into the bathroom as fast as her ankles would allow and had a shower as she tried to calm down both her raging hormones and the butterflies that had taken up permanent residence years ago the first time she had seen him. Suffice to say she failed.

'I'm doomed.'

Realising the following four days were going to be hell, she knew she couldn't kick him out. No matter what happened between them at the end she wanted to spend her last days with him, whether they be pleasant or torturous. She dried herself off, and just in case he was still in the bedroom, she wrapped the towel around herself.

However, when she opened the door he wasn't there.

Although, she did find one of her outfits lying on the bed. She smiled a little. Seemed he wanted her to wear it. So she did.

Sarah hunted for and found appropriate panties and stockings to go with the outfit. She tried the top on first to see if the laces needed readjusting but they were fine. After dressing, she gathered accessories and applied make-up. By that stage her hair had mostly dried in the hair towel, so she scrunched some heat activated mousse through it and blow dried her hair, scrunching it as she went. Then she fluffed her hair about and looked in the mirror.

Hoping for the best, Sarah sighed, grabbed her walking stick then headed out into the kitchen.

She knew where he would be sitting so she didn't look up as she walked into the dining/kitchen area because, as per usual, she was too shy to see his expression immediately. Only she didn't hear a sound of any kind. Wondering if he was in the room at all, she raised her eyes. He was exactly where she thought he would be. His eyes slowly travelled up and down looking her over.

He was stunned. It took a lot of effort on his part to not let his jaw drop to the floor. She looked amazing and he was pleased she had chosen to wear the outfit he had laid out for her.

Whatever she had done to her hair it looked light and fluffy, hair to play with. His eyes slowly travelled down her body. The top was a corset top made of dark blue brocade that had black and silver flowers. The trumpet sleeves were dark blue lace with a scalloped hem that billowed softly around her hands. The front of the corset had a silver busk hook and eye system with the back being a lace up.

Watching her move, while tight, he could see the corset wasn't overly restrictive but then she didn't need it to hold weight in. As he inspected her top he wondered if she was braless or just wearing a strapless. Since the sleeves sat on the edge of her shoulders and were made of lace it was easy to see no other straps under the fabric.

Then he chided himself for the useless thought which would lead nowhere other than another cold shower. However, in the back of his mind he was guessing braless.

The skirt, a high-low, was a multi toned blue velvet that looked like a bad dye job but wasn't. The hem came down to the tops of her low heeled, knee high black velvet boots at the front. It was full with lots of fabric, it flared very well. The back of the skirt had extra fabric so as to not detract from the fullness of the front. That excess material was gathered like a train on a wedding dress and dropped down to her ankles. Over all, the longest part of the skirt was short enough so she couldn't step on it while walking and it swirled around her as she moved.

She had finished the ensemble with a small black shoulder bag with blue flowers and a silver chain strap. Then she looked up and he could see her face. She had makeup on. When she blinked he could see her eyelids were in different shades of blue with a touch of silver and her lips... her lipstick was an amazing colour, a reddish purplish colour. It took him a moment to realise she had a dark blue eyeliner with a little artistic swirl on as well. He was too busy looking at her eye shadow, which obscured the detail of the eyeliner slightly, then at her lips and what he wanted to do to those lusciously berry-like painted lips.

"Stunning. I never knew you were into that style." He said in a rather quiet voice. He couldn't help it. Someone could have drawn a gun and shot him right then and he wouldn't have been able to react in time.

"You really like it?" She murmured in surprise. She didn't have enough sense about her to keep her voice neutral, pleasant.

"Yes I do." His reply was as quiet as his earlier comment and she smiled a little with happiness that he did.

"My husband wasn't into the style and once I had the weight on it didn't seem right to wear it then. When I lost the weight I needed new clothing so I chose this." She said shyly. Then she lifted her skirt to mid-thigh to show off the stockings.

"Noting the breeze out there you will catch glimpses of them so I thought I would show you them now." Her voice faded away like it always did and she blushed profusely while showing him the back of them as well.

'Or are they pantyhose? No. No, I think they would be stockings. The outfit seems to warrant stockings rather than pantyhose. Would be int... No, I am not going to follow that thought or I will need a second, colder, shower.'

Holding the back of her skirt out of the way she also showed him the back of them. Staring at her legs, he admired the design and sheerness of the stockings. They had little black flowers intermittently on them with a solid vine with flowers as the back 'seam'. He thought she was just so sexy. He imagined the 'seam' was from heel to the top of her thigh. To complete the outfit she had a small black shoulder bag with blue flowers and a silver chain strap slung from right shoulder to left hip.

"Nice. Very nice. The outfit looks good on you." He said in that quiet voice again and her butterflies set off in an excited swirling.

Noting the cup of tea and breakfast was there waiting for her, she sat down at the table. After pouring milk and honey on her cereal, she started eating. He joined her in eating his.

She was glad he liked what she was wearing. More than glad, truth be told, but she wanted more from him than just those words. That admission to herself surprised her. She hadn't realised how much she had wanted his approval, his acceptance, of her chosen style. However, she also wanted him to take her in his arms and show her what he thought about her style.

'What a terrible time to discover such a revelation. The timing sucks big time.'

"You obviously know the shops to go to for that particular style of fashion." He commented casually.

"Some, but I made this particular skirt and top." She responded softly. While pleased with her accomplishment, she was embarrassed as well. 'Just once I would like not to be insecure in anything.'

"You made it?" He couldn't help sounding surprised. Somehow she always managed to surprise him at the oddest times.

"Don't sound so incredulous." She grumped at him.

He laughed. "Sorry but I never pictured you sewing at all."

"The same as you didn't picture me singing or playing the

keyboard even though you bought me one." She frowned at him.

He just smiled. "No I didn't."

Then he grabbed the dishes once they had finished, washed them then turned to her. "Come on. We're going out." And, ignoring her stunned look, he just walked out the back door, knowing she would follow. He grinned knowing she couldn't see it.

She shrugged and followed him; which she was happy to do. He was dressed in new mid blue jeans and a short sleeved dark green polo shirt. She loved the way the shirt fitted firmly across his chest. The way it showed off his not quite subtle muscles and the way it moved when he moved. She also liked the way his jeans hugged his waist, hips and thighs.

'Oh, and that arse. So sexy.'

Standing near the jeep waiting for her, the breeze was very accommodating by ruffling her skirt sufficiently he got to see the tops of her stockings and matching lace panties as she descended the stairs. And they were stockings; the garter-less stay-up kind. 'What a delightful view!'

Then he wondered if the panties were actually a g-string. He had bought her a pair last year and he knew she had worn them because they were for the rest of the outfit he had bought for her and she had worn the rest of the outfit. With a private smile to himself they got into the Jeep and he headed towards the city.

Normally he didn't have the radio on but he was hoping she would be relaxed enough to sing. Having the radio on hadn't escaped her notice, as he hadn't done so the last time they had driven together. Nightwish's *'For the Heart I Once Had'* played so she sang it. Since he had heard her sing already she figured it didn't hurt to enjoy herself. She sang others as well while he drove to goodness knows where.

'She still has a lovely voice.' He had missed her beautiful voice, so was pleased when she started to sing.

It wasn't until they were entering the Queensland Museum/State Library car park in South Brisbane did she realise where they were going. She sat up in her seat properly. "The museum?" She asked incredulously.

"I take it you still haven't been to the museum?" He commented with a smile. He remembered it from her 'to do' list that was on the same piece of paper as her 'to get' list.

She gazed at him in surprise, "No." She said softly. She couldn't believe what he was doing for her. She understood, in part at least, why he was doing it but it surprised her none-the-less.

They spend the whole morning exploring the museum. Without thinking, she grabbed his hand as they went from one exhibit to another. His hand was warm in hers and it pleased her immensely that he hadn't tried to reclaim his hand back from her. While he was surprised and delighted when she did so, her fingers lacing with his. He didn't think she realised she'd placed her hand in his. Either way he was happy to be holding her tiny delicate hand.

The place was full of animals, historic items, interactive displays and just so much to see and touch. There were so many interesting facts to read. While he did look at the exhibits with her, he suspected he spent more time watching her.

Watching her eyes light up at the various things they stopped at. Watching her eagerness to point out some fact – she found fascinating – to him. Watching her grow more tired, as her feet hurt – she started limping more when her ankles started hurting, and her ignoring them just so she could play with the next interactive display or see the next curiosity.

The two of them finally left around mid-afternoon. By that stage Sarah fully realised that she was holding his hand, their fingers laced. She gently let go, somewhat reluctantly, blushing slightly. He knew he was a little disappointed when she had. When her stomach rumbled rather loudly, she blushed a little harder and Kaelan laughed as he led her back to the car.

'She certainly has one of the most vocal stomachs I have ever heard.' So he escorted her back to the Jeep so they could find a place to eat.

He opened the door for her, and just before they got in, she suddenly hugged him, "Thank you." She almost whispered.

Despite him having carried her a number of times in the weeks leading up to her becoming a therian, they had never hugged. She was all too aware of everything about him right at that moment and aware of how short she was with the side of her face against his chest. Aware of his steady heartbeat and aware of hers pounding away so fast.

He paused then hugged her in return. "I'm glad you enjoyed it." It took a lot of effort for him to sound calm.

Even though he was there to kill her, perversely, she felt safe in his arms.

'This is the first time we've hugged, held onto each other, while we're both standing and, blast it, she's so tiny. I've always known it but, damn, never like this. Anyone would think she's my little sister. I, for one, am glad she isn't.'

"I did." She smiled. Maybe it was embarrassment, she didn't know, but they cautiously parted.

He didn't know if she held him a little longer than normal or he held her a little longer, but they eventually let go of each other then they got into the Jeep and drove off in silence. He was glad of the distraction of driving because he felt conflicted over his feelings for her and the hit he had to go through with, because he knew if he didn't someone else would.

'Especially if the one who placed the contract isn't found.' It was a possibility he didn't like admitting; even to himself.

A few minutes later Kaelan managed to find a suitable café. He told her to find a seat while he grabbed a couple of menus. When he reached her Sarah had found the perfect table, leaving him with the best seat with his back to a solid wall, but leaving her back exposed. He gazed at her.

"Was this table choice deliberate?"

She gazed up at him shyly and nodded. The table she chose sat in the corner of two solid opaque walls with his seat against one of the opaque walls so his back wasn't exposed. Just the way he liked it.

He sat down. "This is the second time you have chosen a table with me in mind. Why?" He didn't know why but he had to try to understand why she did it.

She shrugged, "I don't know really. It seemed right." Then stared down at her hands. Out of her peripheral vision she could see him shake his head.

'There's more to it than what she's saying.' He peered around the inside of the café then motioned to a couple on the other side of the room. Based on the little things he had witnessed since meeting her, he decided to test her.

"Tell me what you see about them."

She peered over at them, "My guess would be that they work together. He really likes her but she doesn't feel the same way about him."

'Interesting.' He thought then asked. "Why do you say that?"

"Well, they're both in business suits, he's leaning on the table towards her but she is sitting back away from him. She doesn't want to seem confrontational or closed off, as in unfriendly, which is why she continually uncrosses her arms and looks at him occasionally without any hostility of any kind. She wants to be friends but nothing more, while he wants the more."

"How do you know that's what they are doing?" He couldn't keep the curiosity from his voice.

"I don't I guess. It is just a guess based on how they're reacting to each other. She's not angry at him like a lover might be if they were having a disagreement and he isn't pleading with her as a lover would under the same circumstances. Of course I could be totally wrong, it happens."

"Okay. What about that couple out there?" He pointed to another man and woman who were sitting at a table outside the café itself near the footpath. He indicated to another man and woman who were sitting at a table outside the café itself near the footpath.

She turned around to look at them then turned back to him;

much better to look at. "They work together, not lovers."

"Explain." Her instant response confused him. 'How can she be so sure?'

She looked at the pair again.

"While they might be acting like lovers, they aren't. Yes they're both leaning towards each other and their hands are next to each other's but they aren't touching in any way; just the illusion of touching. Their smiles seem to be plastered in place so looks sort of fake, using an economy of words and lip movement when they talk. They look like they're undercover actually." She turned back to face Kaelan.

"Explain." He said again. 'She truly is more observant than I had originally thought.'

"They're both positioned so both ends of the road can be monitored and they are monitoring their designated lines of sight with very little deviation. Also, I'm not sure but it almost looks like he might have a gun under his left arm, it's the only thing I can think of for a bulge under the jacket that high. But what do I know. I could be wrong about them as well." She said as she shrugged in a depreciative way.

'I can't believe my ears. Is it just some ability she's managed to pick up or has she truly been trained and is hiding it from me? Just when I thought I had her figured out.'

"I don't think you are wrong about either couple and yes he does have a gun under his left arm. How did you do that?"

"I don't know. I've sort of always been able to do it. As I said I don't always get it right and there are some I can't do it with at all and I'm no good at working it out if I'm involved in the equation." She looked down at her hands, embarrassed at having revealed more than she intended.

For some reason, although true to form, she was embarrassed as she stared at her hands. 'Why? Is she embarrassed for the last part of her comment or for having revealed so much about herself? What did she just reveal? Unfortunately things are moving a little too quickly to decipher this so soon. But her ability is just instinct?'

"Don't be upset Sarah. I just think it's amazing. However, I do think it's a bit careless of you to place your back to any open space like that."

She was suddenly angry and she leant back away from him.

"Great! I give you what you want and you call me careless. Fine!" She then stood up, bumped into a couple of chairs behind her in her haste, walked out the door and disappearing from sight as she headed in the direction away from the Jeep.

She couldn't believe it. She had tried to do something nice for him and he criticised her for it. However, deliberately heading away from the jeep, she should have realised she wouldn't have gotten far before he caught up to her. Even though she had gotten further that time than she had over a year ago.

Sitting there watching her, he frowned at her choice of direction then went after her. Not hurrying because he knew she wouldn't be too far ahead he was, however, surprised at how far she'd managed to get by the time he had caught up with her. With his long legs, he still didn't have to run to catch up to her though. He grabbed at her arm to stop her from going any further. Her expression was not friendly.

She glared up at him when his hand gripped her upper arm.

She went still then stared at his hand.

"I'm sorry Sarah. Habits die hard."

She looked up at him, craning her neck back to do so as her eyes went wide, "Habits? What habits Kaelan? We don't have any habits together for them to be hard to die." She cried softly in exasperation. It couldn't be about safety since he was there to kill her so she had no idea what in the hell he was referring to.

'Huh? Okay, I'm confused. What is she referring to? I was just commenting about my standard protection/security measures that are automatic to me.' He frowned at her as he tried to work out what was said and what went wrong and where. He let her go.

"Come home with me please." He said when he couldn't figure out the problem quickly enough. 'Blast it! She's just so damned confusing!'

Just like that, without saying another word or waiting for him, she turned around and started walking back towards the Jeep. They passed the undercover couple. Kaelan and Sarah had noticed the undercover couple watching them and they both heard the woman murmur as they passed the table.

"Lover's tiff."

'Like she knows what she's talking about, the silly woman.' Sarah thought snarkily to herself.

'Lover's tiff?! Really?! Highly unlikely! Emotional, obstinate and a general pain in the arse female, yes! That I'll believe.' Kaelan muttered mentally to himself.

Once in the Jeep and on the road again...

"Why didn't you protect yourself first, Sarah?" He asked with a frown without taking his eyes off the road.

Suddenly she was exasperated again. 'So it was about safety after all? UGH!'

"You can't leave it alone can you? Fine! Ignoring the fact that you prefer to sit with a solid non-see-through wall at your back, I figured that you would be able to react far faster than I ever could. You were the better choice for protecting me than me protecting you or even myself. There, satisfied?"

She slumped down in her seat feeling as if the day was coming to a horrible end. Once again she had to fight off the tears. Thankfully they were only a half-hearted attempt so she was successful.

"You really thought that?" Her answer surprised him and it was actually a good choice based on her reasoning. He just sat there with his mouth open as he drove.

For once, him being surprised about her annoyed her. "Pick your jaw off the floor, a truck could drive into it." She muttered at him.

It was obvious she was still upset with him. He snapped his mouth shut then started chuckling.

"That's funny." And every time he thought about her comment he just kept chuckling for a short while longer. He noticed her turning her head away to look out the window beside her. He was sorry he had upset her since she hadn't really done anything wrong.

Unfortunately, or fortunately for him, she couldn't stay mad at him. She had to turn her head away so he couldn't see her smile. She loved his smile and when he chuckled and laughed. Then her stomach growled rather loudly in protest of her walking out of the café without feeding it.

He laughed again. It seemed, to her, that her loudly grumbling stomach always amused him. He decided to put her stomach out of its misery and went through the second drive-thru they came across; because she didn't like the products of the first one. They bought burgers, chips and drinks, with a dessert for her and ate them on the way home.

When they got home he asked her to sing and play the keyboard for him. He did so in an effort to make up to her for criticising her. He asked so nicely that she did so and it pleased him. No love songs though which was a shame because he did enjoy them and imagined she was singing them to him. After a while she had to stop, because she was so tired that she was making mistakes. So, she went into the bedroom, changed into the boxer briefs and tank top and crawled into bed. It didn't take long for her to fall asleep.

He went to the spare room to check the tracker program. He also looked at other jobs and checked the status of her hit. It was still listed as claimed so no one else would try to take her out. The last thing he needed was the guy who ordered the hit to become impatient and relist it. A couple of hours later he headed to bed.

He laid there for a while just staring up at the darkened ceiling and listened to her breathe. She woke up briefly, vaguely noted he was beside her, rolled towards him then went back to sleep. He fell asleep to the sound of her breathing.

Somewhere between one and two in the morning, Sarah crawled out of bed and went into the kitchen. Turning on a light, she set about making herself a toasted sandwich from some leftover bacon, minute steak, egg, cheese and tomatoe. After having fried the bacon, steak and egg, she layered them with the tomatoe and cheese on the bread. While it was toasting, she made herself a hot chocolate.

"Sarah, are you alright?"

She let out a squeak of fright and was glad she wasn't holding onto anything hot. "Geez! Stop sneaking up on me..."

"Damn! I'm sorry..."

Both exclaimed at the same time. Then she ducked her head and chuckled.

"Honestly Kaelan, you have to stop sneaking around. You're at home for goodness sake. But, yes, I'm just hungry."

"I see and I wasn't sneaking." He stated with a hint of amusement.

She crossed her arms under her breasts. "Oh yes you were..." She paused then her eyes widened as two and two started coming together. "You rotter!"

He stared at her in surprise. Her response wasn't one he was expecting. He also had to keep his desire in check as her breasts rose and became more pronounced with her action. "Excuse me?"

"You've been practicing. Ever since that night you left here last year, you didn't like the fact that I had heard you coming up behind me. So, you've been practicing in creeping about." She shook her head incredulously then turned back to her waiting food. Grabbing it, she took it to the table.

"Well, I am a hunter and I can't let the monsters get the better of me because I can't move quietly." His grin disappeared as he realised what he had just said.

Her smile also vanished as she sat down.

"Sarah, I'm sorry. I didn't mean…" He was worried about her believing he saw her that way. He sat opposite her.

'Despite what she is, I don't see her as a monster. Far from it. From everything I have heard and seen about her, both over the past year and in the past day, she hasn't changed regardless of the disease.'

She shook her head. "It's okay. I knew what you meant." She responded quietly. She wanted to believe he didn't really see her that way. She really did. However, she did see herself like that and found it difficult to believe that he wouldn't.

'Damn it, but I'm going to have to change the way I think. It's bad enough I'm responsible for what she is that I don't need to insult her or make her feel worse. It's not her fault.' Then she broke into his thoughts.

"Would you like some?" She asked softly as she indicated to her sandwich she had just cut in half.

"Yeah, sure." He responded slowly as her offer had surprised him. He reached for one half and her cup. He took a sip, only to flinch over how sweet it was. Gazing at her as he handed her cup back, he saw her smile at his reaction. He took a bite of the sandwich, which was almost half of it, then placed it back on her plate.

"You don't like it?" She asked in surprise around the bite he had just taken. She couldn't imagine him not liking it with what she's seen him eat during the times they've been around each other.

"Yeah I do but I'm not really that hungry. Only came out because I was surprised to find you not in bed and was concerned something was wrong."

"Oh okay. Yeah, sometimes I get hungry during the night. Part and parcel of my now faster metabolism." She thought it was nice he would be concerned over her, regardless of what he had to do in a few days' time.

He nodded. It wasn't like there was much he could say to that. But what came out of her mouth next surprised him.

"You know I have no problems with your chosen career, but why did you leave the Army and become a hunter?"

Nodding, Kaelan realised he had the perfect opportunity to tell her about his past yet, at the same time, it wasn't the right moment. Instead, he gave her part of the truth.

"I discovered I was good at hunting the rogues and they were more of a challenge than what I was doing for the Army. Plus I do enjoy it as well." He watched her reaction as she slowly nodded.

"It's good you enjoy it and are good at it because we need people like you to keep us safe from the rogues." She stated quietly.

Her statement took him by surprise and he didn't know how to respond to it. So they lapsed into silence while she finished her snack. Then she placed her dishes on the sink and they headed back to bed. It wasn't long before she fell asleep and him not long after.

Chapter 15

During the night Kaelan had rolled over so he was facing Sarah. He awoke to feel her breath against his bare chest so warm. It took a moment to realise she was still asleep. However, they were separated by her body pillow with her arm resting on top of it and its hand tucked under her chin. Daringly, he allowed himself to play with her hair. Even sleep tousled it was so soft. His face was so close to her head that he could have kissed her.

Instead, he watched his breath flutter strands of her hair. He wanted to do more, he wanted to hold her, he wanted to love her. Instead he settled for just playing with her hair and enjoying the feel of her breath lightly caressing his skin. He was grateful for the body pillow between them as it would hide his arousal from her.

Suddenly, her breathing changed. She was waking up. His fingers twitched with the effort to stop them from playing with her hair. He felt her move ever so minutely then she breathed against his chest. He closed his eyes at the sensation and of how erotic that simple action had felt.

Sarah awoke to the feel of a warm breath on the top of her head and fingers twitching, moving, slightly in her hair. She opened her eyes and was greeted with the sight of Kaelan's smooth, scar-less patch of bare chest near her face. Not that she cared about his scars as they proved he was both a fighter and survivor.

Softly she breathed against it and felt her breath gently bounce back at her and the spicy smell of him wafted back. She closed her eyes wanting to touch him, to wrap her arms around him but she couldn't. She wasn't strong enough to overcome her shyness.

'Besides, I'll be dead soon so why bother torturing myself more than I already am.'

"Morning." Kaelan murmured.

"Morning." She said so softly it was almost a whisper. She was embarrassed as if she had been sprung staring at him. 'Well, I guess I sort of had been.'

'She's still very much the baby bunny I'd left over a year ago.' He reluctantly rolled onto his back, stretched and decided to go have a rather cool shower.

She almost echoed him. She did roll onto her back and stretch but she just sat on the edge of the bed instead as he walked around the bed towards the en suite. "If you don't mind, I would like to stay home instead of going out today until the night of the full moon please."

He gazed down at her, but she was staring at the floor. 'I guess I can't blame her for not wanting to be social right now as the time left ticks away.' "Your choice Sarah." Then he entered the bathroom.

When he came out, she went in. He noticed she refused to look at him whenever he came out. He had thought it was just yesterday after she had touched his scar and was embarrassed about it. However it seemed to be more than that. He just stared at the closed bathroom door for a few minutes.

'I think I'm no longer confused about how I feel about her, but that can always change. One never knows with her.' He sighed as he then remembered why he was there.

'This is one of the rare times I really hate my job, but a promise is a promise. In all honesty, there is no way I would let anyone else kill her. It's the one reason why I'm tracking the money back to the one who'd placed the hit. Maybe she'll be able to talk them into cancelling it. Damn, who am I trying to convince? I don't believe she'll be successful. I guess all I can do is make the remaining time as pleasant as possible.'

As he grabbed clothing for himself, he picked one of her long dresses in a nice muted green. The top half of the dress seemed to be made of a lighter weight brocade-like fabric compared to the corset she wore the previous day and it laced up the front this time with cord of the same colour. The skirt of the dress, which appeared to be floor length, was the same colour but seemed to be light weight cotton.

'Very pretty dress.' He mused and left the room.

He turned the stereo on while heading to the kitchen. He made breakfast for them both and a cuppa when he heard the shower turn off.

When he came out wrapped in a towel, she went in for her shower. She was so embarrassed at her behaviour that she couldn't look at him. Seeing him wrapped in just a towel that sat low on the hips each morning was of no help either. Sure he looked wonderful but she couldn't do anything about it, that and the fact that he didn't love her.

'Every time I think my life is settling into something good, something else comes alone and kicks me in the teeth. Only, this time, there's no recovering from it.' She thought sadly.

Again, he wasn't in the room when she came out and again she found one of her outfits on the bed waiting. It was just one of her around the house dresses. The bodice and sleeves were a slightly darker sage green, light weight brocade that laced up at the front with matching green cord. The skirt of the dress was the same colour sage green but in a cotton fabric slightly thicker than cheese cloth. Privately, she was pleased he wanted to see her in her particular style of clothing that she happily wore them for him.

He was sitting at the table when he saw her come out to the main part of the house. She heard Gary Moore's *'Over the Hills and Far Away'* playing on the stereo and moved to stand by it. Then she just started singing softly, doing gentle keyboard actions in time with the music. She so loved that song. Nightwish's version was okay but Gary's was better.

Watching her, he was suddenly in two minds about her singing. 'I don't want to hear her sing anymore because in two days' time I never will again. At the same time, because I will never be hearing her sing again, I want her to sing while she can.'

He sighed and decided to just enjoy it while he could. 'May as well since I'm sort of responsible in encouraging her to sing in the first place.' He got up and stood behind her.

"Like the song huh?" His amused voice commented behind her.

She jumped then smiled sheepishly at him. "Yeah."

"Come have breakfast. Nice dress, you make that one?" He noted her bare feet with a smile.

While Kaelan was dressed in a grey t-shirt that fitted him snugly and a pair of faded grey jeans. Nothing on the feet, but then there was nothing on hers either. He looked very yummy indeed. She mentally chided herself over her thoughts. What was the point of them when she would be dead soon?

"Thank you and no, shop bought." She followed him to the table where their breakfast was waiting. They ate then did the dishes together, he washed and she dried.

After pouring a bit of detergent into the water, Kaelan decided to try for the bubbles Sarah had created the last time she had done the dishes. He wanted to see her face with the bubbles all around her. Apparently, though, he wasn't doing it right when none came out when he squeezed the bottle. She smiled then leant in against him. His breath caught in his throat and his heart stuttered a little and couldn't help but notice her breast pressed against his arm as she reached across him. She felt so warm and inviting and his body reacted accordingly.

However, it appeared he had the lid open too far because she closed it then popped it open just a little. She placed her hand over his then gave the practiced, slower, squeeze so he could feel the pressure and speed she used. He thought his body was going to go into a meltdown and it took a lot of effort to concentrate on what they were doing instead on just her.

So he tried again, but it seemed he still wasn't doing it right as she giggled and showed him how to do it again a few more times. He had actually gotten it on the first demonstration she had given him. He was initially just teasing her, not that she knew he was, but then he liked her leaning against him with her hand on his.

'So soft and gentle.'

After great pretence at learning how to do it right he finally did so, just for her. But also because the tightness in the crotch of his jeans were making him more than slightly uncomfortable. 'I have to or I'll end up doing something so un-gentlemanly she'll end up hating me for sure.'

Suffice to say, it did take a while to get the dishes done but there were bubbles everywhere and she was smiling. At the end of the dishes, he ran his hand over her hair to pop some of the bubbles lingering around her, which was a good excuse for him to touch her hair while she was awake.

Her heart almost stopped when she saw him smiling with bubbles all around them, he looked wonderful and, for just a little while, the lines of stress around his eyes, mouth and brow were gone. She also liked it when he touched her hair. His touch was so light it was like a caress.

Not once did she think him a dunce for not comprehending how to do it as it allowed her to touch him. It took her a little practice to get those bubbles after all. 'Why is it I can do this but I can't tell him how I feel about him? Sure I'm still shy but this is different.' She had no answer.

After the dishes were done she went into the sitting room, grabbed a book she'd been reading and settled into her favourite of the single-seaters. There were two single-seaters and a three-seater futon in the room with all the bookcases. Kaelan came in a moment or two later looking around the room.

'She's bought more since I last saw her collection. I'd been surprised when I saw her collection back when I first packed them up to be moved here. Not because she read but because of the wide variety her collection consisted of. Such a wide variety. Huh. She's also bought new bookcases to match the ones I'd bought for her. I wonder what she did with hers.' Then he remembered the one he saw in the spare bedroom and wondered if the others were in the other two rooms.

He stood in front of one of the bookcases after a particular novel caught his attention. He grabbed Tom Clancy's 'Rainbow Six' and turned to face her. "Have you read all these?" He indicated to all the books.

"No, not all. The bookcase behind you and those over there I haven't read any yet." She said indicating to them in turn. Danny's books just so happened to be included in the unread selection.

"So you haven't read this book yet." Motioning to the book in his hand.

"Not yet unfortunately." She was sad about it because now she would never have the time to read it.

"I have to say I'm surprised that you have something like this in your collection. I wouldn't have thought it was your speed."

"Well, I saw the movie a few years ago, on dvd, and decided to get the book. The books do tend to be better than the movies most of the time regardless how good the movies are." She said quietly.

He sat down in the other single-seater facing the one she was in. If she had known he would join her, she would have sat on the futon in the hopes he would sit on it with her. 'Oh well, maybe tomorrow.'

Flicking through the pages, glancing at bits here and there, closed the book to look at the back cover, and opened it again at the beginning. He decided to read it to her. 'I remember, on that list of wants and to dos of hers, one of the items was to be read to.'

He remembered reading the book years ago and remembered enjoying it. 'I didn't get to see the movie though. I rarely do since my job keeps me away most of the time, which is more my choice, fault, than anything else I guess.' He opened the book at the beginning then started reading out loud...

Rainbow Six

Prologue

Setting Up

John Clark had more time in airplanes than most licensed pilots, and he knew the statistic as well as any of them, but he still didn't like the idea of crossing the ocean on a twin-engine airliner. Four was the right number of engines, he thought, because losing one meant losing only 25 percent of the aircraft's available power, whereas on this United 777, it meant losing half...

He noted her closing her book and sat there watching him as he read. A slight smile caressed her lips as she listened to the story. Then she settled further into the chair and closed her eyes. He read for a little while longer before stopping.

Sarah closed the book she had opened and sat there listening to him read. She had never been read to before and he knew it because it had been on the same list as the keyboard and the museum visit. She didn't know what to think of his effort to make any one of them come true for her, but it pleased her to say the least.

At first she was more interested in hearing his voice, listening to it rise and fall with the telling of the story. He read very well and had a wonderful voice to listen to. However, after a while she actually started listening to the story itself. Settling back into the chair she listened to the story, closing her eyes. In her mind she could see the movie playing. Sometimes it would stutter when a part in the book wasn't in the movie or had been changed enough that the two didn't quite match.

No sooner had he ceased reading than her eyes were open and looking at him in confusion. "Why did you stop?"

"I thought you had fallen asleep." He responded gently. 'Not that I would have minded if she had been. I would have been just as happy to sit there and watch her do that as well. Hell! She could have been sewing and I would have watched her.'

"Oh, no. I was enjoying it, seeing scenes from the movie. Please, continue." She blushed and he resumed. She couldn't help but get caught up in the story; she was enjoying it that much.

So he continued to read. Every now and then he would catch

a slight smile or small frown flit across her face and watched her tense up as she listened to the story. 'Seems she may have a hell of an imagination. She's certainly becoming involved in the story from what I can see.'

He stopped reading when her stomach started to voice its opinion. He was pleased to see her eating regularly and decently. She made lunch which consisted of sliced fried kabana and home-made potatoe salad with bacon, shallots, a mild tasting mayonnaise and sour cream in it. After lunch, he continued reading the book until dinner time then the pair cooked together.

About half way through a dinner of beef stroganoff with mashed potatoes and slices of buttered crusty bread roll...

"How is the search for the person who ordered the hit going?" She asked softly. She was afraid he wouldn't find them, or at least not in time. She didn't really want to bring up the subject but she needed to know what was happening.

Kaelan paused in eating, "The tracking program I'm using is following the money trail and it is leading somewhere. If intelligent enough, the person ordering the hit will hide their tracks by bouncing the money through various sources. The more sources, the longer it takes to trace them. Seems this person is reasonably intelligent, which is an unfortunate disadvantage to us in this instance. I just don't know if it will find the originator in time." He responded quietly. There was nothing much else he could say about it to help her in any way.

She just nodded. His last comment made it seem like he had read her mind. They lapsed back into silence.

After dinner, with his encouragement, she sang and played

the keyboard. A few hours later, they went to bed. He didn't fall asleep until after she had.

*

It seemed like he kept waking up before she did each morning and he was surprised to discover that sometime during the night he had draped his arm around her waist. It took a lot of willpower to just lay there and not move and to keep his breathing normal. However, it was rather difficult as every intake of breath drew her scent of roses – that was the body wash she used – into him, because what he wanted to do was hold her tightly against him.

Then her breathing started to change as she woke up.

Consciousness swam slowly towards the light and as it did she felt a weight around her waist. Sarah was immediately awake with her breath stuck in her throat.

'I know it was accidental, something he'd done in his sleep, but, far out space cookies, do I wish it was something more than wishful thinking on my part.' She also had to restrain herself from holding his arm to her.

"Morning." He murmured behind her.

"Morning." She said softly. "I guess my breathing gave me away." She couldn't get her voice any louder. 'I so hate being shy.'

"Yeah, it did." He sounded like he was amused by it. He smiled even though she couldn't see it. 'Yet, she doesn't complain about my arm being around her and that surprises me.'

As she started to roll onto her back, he reluctantly removed his arm from around her. 'I know, I'm basically torturing myself with these little things since she doesn't love me and because she will be no more all too soon, but I can't help it. Or, maybe that's the point, I don't want to help it, don't want to fight it.' He mentally sighed as he got out of bed and headed to the shower.

When he removed his arm, 'Can't say I'm not disappointed, far from it actually.' She thought sadly.

They repeated the routine of the past couple of mornings and met him in the kitchen for breakfast.

The pair started what was becoming a routine of breakfast, dishes with plenty of bubbles to hear her laugh. This time she curled up at one end of the futon, so he sat at the other end. Her choice of seating pleased him because it meant they were nearer to each other.

With both of them on the futon this time, she was so pleased he had joined her. Then he resumed reading Tom Clancy's 'Rainbow Six'. This time they stocked themselves with drinks and nibblies so her stomach wouldn't interrupt the reading session. He didn't complain about the snacks as they were a mix of healthy and not healthy.

In their own private thoughts, both realised they wouldn't get to finish the book before tomorrow night; that she wouldn't get to know how it ended. The only reason she let him continue was so they could be together and she could listen to his wonderful voice. While Kaelan came to a decision.

'I don't think I could ever finish this book once she's gone. I will never read this book ever again.'

The pair did pause for lunch then continued the read-a-thon till dinner. After dinner – which he fried some fish and julienned vegetables for them both and she served up a cake she'd baked at some point before he had arrived, they sat in the lounge room and he listened to her sing and play the keyboard. They called it quits again when she started making obvious mistakes.

Following the singing and keyboard playing session, she noted Kaelan checking the laptop while she headed to the bedroom for some sleep. She slept because she was so tired but her last thought was that tomorrow was the night of the full moon and her last night alive. She curled up under the covers and couldn't stop the tears from flowing. She didn't actually cry, the tears just leaked out.

By the time he came to bed she was already asleep. However, he could see tears drying on her face. 'Like me, she knows time is running out and there's nothing either of us can do about it.'

Standing there, he just watched her for a few minutes as she slept before he finally crawled into bed and spooned her as best he could. 'Not easy with such height differences between the two of us; she's 156cm and I'm 193cm, as well as her being so high up in the bed.' After much repositioning – how he never woke her up he would never know – he had managed and fell asleep with his left arm around her waist and his right above her head with his fingers lightly playing with her hair.

*

Sometime during the night he had rolled away from her, but he hadn't minded because Sarah had rolled over and had moved up against him. Her body was a warm line along the back of his and her arm resting on his side with her hand against his chest. Kaelan was just disappointed it was something that happened during her sleep rather than a conscious action on her part.

However, he revelled in it while he could. When she moved he then discovered he couldn't feel her piercings and realised they would have been removed when she first became a therian and could never have them again. That, too, disappointed him because he never got the chance to play with them.

'They were just so cute.'

Then it occurred to him that the body pillow wasn't between them. Her hand twitched then she was awake. Her breath sighed warmly against his skin.

During the night sometime Sarah had obviously rolled over and snuggled closer to Kaelan because her arm was draped across his lower chest. Of course it would be something she would do in her sleep, of all the times to not be shy. She hadn't realised it at first until her hand had twitched and brushed against his bare skin.

She wanted to do more but couldn't. 'Why do I have to be so shy? I hate being shy but I don't know how not to be.' She sighed knowing she sounded like a broken down record. Slowly she removed her arm from him, making the sensation of their skin touching last as long as possible – which wasn't all that long because of her short arms – since it was their last time together like that.

What also surprised her was the lack of body pillow. She hadn't slept without it since the accident that damaged her ankles. She knew she had gone to sleep with it but didn't know where it was right then. When she rolled away from him, pain shot through her ankles due to the lack of support during the night. Hence the reason for the body pillow.

When she removed her arm, gently dragging it across his skin, he didn't know if it was deliberate on her part or not. However, it took a lot of effort on his not to take hold of her hand and keep it there. Let alone roll her on her back and claim her right then. Instead, "You alright?"

"Sorry, I didn't mean to wake you." She whispered as she fought back the tears.

He rolled over and looked at her. "I wasn't asleep."

Eyes down so he wouldn't see her tears, she nodded. Sitting up, after he had entered the en suite, she sat there so she would be able to walk without her walking stick and saw her body pillow half in and half out of the bed. With a shake of her head, she dragged it back where it belonged.

Once in the shower, he cursed himself for his stupidity. For allowing those little moments to happen. For staying there when his head had told him not to when he had arrived three nights ago because it had just made his job that much harder.

'However, maybe I deserve it since it's my fault for where we both have ended up. How could I let a little slip of a girl like her get past my barriers like that? How had it happened? Why her and no other woman? After all these years I still don't know.'

He scrubbed himself vigorously in frustration as he tried to rid himself of those useless repetitive thoughts.

'Damn, but I'm so stupid. I should have stayed away. I should never have taken her with me on that hit a year ago. I shouldn't have been so damned selfish and protected her instead.' He sighed at those same old hopeless thoughts then finished his shower.

When it was her turn in the shower she gave in to the tears and cried. Despite the pair of them getting upset with each other at the beginning she had enjoyed the past three days. She had sort of hoped that if they ever got together then that would be how their time together would be like... enjoying each other's company.

'Why did I have to fall in love with him? Tonight, it all comes to an end. Forever. No matter what, I still prefer him to be the one to kill me than anyone else. But no matter what I wouldn't change anything except to tell him that I love him. Now it's too late.'

She took a little longer going out to the kitchen in the hopes of easing some of the redness in her eyes from the crying. Unfortunately it was taking too long, so red eyes and all, she went to have breakfast.

"You've been crying?" He inquired quietly, not that he blamed her.

'Figures.' She thought then responded, "No, I got shampoo in my eyes. The damn thing stings like crazy no matter how quickly you wash it out."

"Uhuh, that's your story and you're sticking to it right?" He felt his lips twitched in amusement. He teased her but he let her have her little lie.

"Yep." She said quietly. 'He obviously knows I'm lying which also figures.'

Repeating the events of the past two days, they went into the sitting room, after breakfast, stocked with food and drink. Sitting on the futon again, Kaelan continued to read to her.

'Just a shame it's taken twenty-seven years before I got to experience it.' She thought to herself. Sarah tried to lose herself in the story but the fact that it was her last day to live prevented her from doing so completely.

Lunch came and went, she wasn't hungry, and still he read. Dinner came but she wasn't hungry then either. While her appetite plummeted, her nervousness slowly grew. She didn't know what to expect, come the evening. Sure, she knew he would make it a quick clean kill, but she didn't know how he would do it. Over the past few days, she had managed to not think about it. As darkness gradually descended, it was all she could think about.

It was almost 8pm when his laptop chimed. Her heart was in her throat. He glanced at her quickly and noted how nervous she had just become then headed to the spare room. She couldn't sit there. She went out on the back verandah to see a deer grazing at the tree line before disappearing back into the bushland. The top rim of the moon was just revealing itself above the immediate horizon.

Settling the laptop, he clicked the active flag. He frowned as he recognised the name.

'Looks like I'll have a second hit after all because there will be no way in hell she'll get him to call it off. Why? What has she done to him? My sources said she's basically been keeping to herself. While I'm not exactly happy about this job, I know I'm going to enjoy this little bonus immensely. He's not going to see dawn.'

He walked back to the sitting room but she wasn't there. Noting the french doors were open, he went out onto the back verandah and saw her standing there staring out into the darkness.

"Sarah."

She jumped at the sound of her name. She just looked up at him with her hands at her side and her breathing a little fast which matched the pounding of her heart.

Just like that, the frightened tiny baby bunny was back when she jumped at the sound of his voice. This time round he didn't like seeing that bunny look on her face.

"The person behind the money is Jonathon Sutterton."

She frowned slightly as she looked down at the floor, then staggered back a step or two. He had to grab her to keep her from falling over. Despite the improvement to her walking she was still unsteady when stepping backwards. Seemed she didn't know why he would order a hit on her either.

She couldn't breathe properly. 'Why? Why would Jonathon do this?'

"Sarah, are you alright?" He didn't even try to keep the worry from his voice.

She gave a small laugh but it had a slight hysterical sound to it with fear and tears mixed in. She bit her bottom lip to stop the sound because she hated it. 'Am I alright he asks. Of course not!'

It was only his promise to her which stopped him from comforting her. He watched her as she took a shaky breath in and let it out slowly. Then she turned and was about to walk away to go inside when he gently grabbed her arm.

"Sarah, look at me." He said firmly.

'Despite what I have to do in a few hours, I can't let her leave like this even though I know I have to.'

She glanced at him quickly but looked away. Her eyes wouldn't settle on anything for too long. "I... I... have a meeting to attend. I'll see you at the range at midnight. I'll be there regardless of the outcome." She said distractedly and pulled away from him.

'What's going through her mind? If only she would talk to me. If I didn't know any better I would say she was in shock. Could she be?'

Starting to walk away she stopped then gazed up at him. "Do you have a number he can call you on to cancel the hit if I'm successful in talking him out of it?" She asked so softly her voice was barely above a whisper. She could feel the tears but fought to stop them from falling.

He stared down at her, frowning because there was nothing he could do to help her then went inside to write a number down for her. She followed him inside but headed to the bedroom to change. She put another dress on but one more appropriate for going among the public in; and dying in, and grabbed her cheap walking stick instead of her good one. When she came out, she grabbed her gloves and helmet.

Once done, he found her standing in the lounge room. She almost seemed child-like standing there looking rather lost. She suspected she looked how she felt despite knowing what she was supposed to do, when Kaelan came towards her. He handed her a plain piece of card. She took it, looked at it and saw a number and nothing else on it.

'Not that it needs anything else on it I guess.'

"Thank you. My will is in the drawer of the dressing table. I've left it for you to deal with it. It tells everything I want done including the dealing with my... body." She paused. She wanted to say so much more and she knew, by her indecisive actions, that it showed. She eventually turned away and walked out the door and headed to Jonathon's place.

His chest tightened with her words.

He just stood there watching her leave. He didn't move until he couldn't hear her scooter any more. So, he decided to take his frustrations out on the gym equipment downstairs in the hopes of filling enough time and to keep his mind from hoping she would be successful.

'Successful or not, Jonathon Sutterton is dead.'

Chapter 16

The moon was rising steadily slowly towards its zenith, full and heavy and lighting up the night brilliantly. Too brightly for the way she felt. She had to admit she didn't know how she managed to get to Jonathon's place in one piece and alive. She didn't really remember the trip there.

'Thank goodness it's night time even if it is the end of the week. Most are either at home already or won't go out for a few more hours yet. Either way, it means less traffic. Well, a little less anyway.' She was admitted entry to the property. She made her way to the back of the house; only they weren't there.

"They have gone to the private meeting place Miss. You know the way I believe." The butler said kindly to her.

"Thank you Malcolm." She smiled a little at him.

He had always been nice to her. While it might have just been his job, she thought it might have been because she was nice to him. Hence why she never corrected his appellation to her.

Then she made her way to the bushland at the back of the property with the moonlight guiding her until she entered the tree line. She was surprised they were back there already. They never were whenever she had been with them.

Once inside the tree line the light dimmed and the air was still. Not even a slight breeze stirred. The further in she went, the darker it got. Every other time she had traipsed through those trees she had been in jaguar form. She took the way slowly. It took longer to get there but she finally made it with no scratches or tears in the dress. With the trees much closer, the moon shone through the upper sections of them creating branchy shadows across the clearing.

"Sarah, what a pleasant surprise." Jonathon greeted as if he was blessed to see her there. What an act.

She gazed around at everyone and saw they were still in human form. Although, it was still a little early yet before they would change if they stuck to Jonathon's time table.

"I wish I could say the same Jonathon. Why?" She didn't clarify because she knew he would understand exactly what she was talking about.

"Why what, Sarah? I don't understand what..." He started, acting innocent and confused regarding her question.

"Don't! You see, the one who took the hit happens to be a friend of mine. I had asked him many months ago to take the job should it ever arise. When he arrived in town to let me know, I asked him to find the person behind the money. Imagine my surprise... my shock... my horror to discover it was you who ordered my death." She started shaking. 'How I hate confrontations.'

"How dare you?!" Lucidia demanded. Under the circumstances she had a right to be angry at Sarah's accusation.

"Sarah, what are you talking about?" Maria exclaimed, horror spreading across her attractive face.

"Jonathon, is this true?" Antonio asked, anger distorting his handsome face as he stood up and moved towards Sarah to stand at her side. It surprised Sarah that he readily believed her when no one else seemed to. At the same time, it pleased her immensely.

Everyone else behind her stayed quiet, watching, waiting. Tonight, they had a new form of entertainment and they eagerly awaited its outcome.

All three questions were asked at the same time. The entire time, Sarah just stared at Jonathon, ignoring everyone else. Except Antonio, as he stepped up beside her, but she didn't look at him. She gradually took a deep breath and let it out just as slowly.

"I deserve the truth before I go meet with him so he can fulfil your order, Jonathon." She said calmly, and suddenly she did feel calm.

'Weird huh?' She had surprised herself since she had just been shaking moments ago.

Abruptly, he and the air around him changed. Slowly, gracefully and menacingly he leant forward and if looks could kill then Sarah would be dead right then.

"I could not risk you rising in the ranks to challenge me, to try and take over the leopards and therefore the control of the League. You have turned out to be more powerful than I ever suspected you to be. Your voice causing others to rise against me proved to be a major threat. So, like any strong leader I decided to eliminate any possible threat to my continual leadership. Meaning you." His voice and face was so full of scorn and hatred. Of her.

The reaction, over the confirmation from Jonathon's own lips, from the rest of the leopards was one of shock. Lucidia stepped back from her husband and rage darkened Antonio's features.

"You stupid fool!" Sarah cried softly in exasperation, "Did it not occur to you to ask me what my goals were? I'm not even a leopard so I can't take leadership of the lepe. I can't challenge you. I can't even rise in rank in the lepe because I am not a part of the Lepe! I don't even have any interest in taking control of the League. If you weren't so damned power hungry and actually just asked me, we wouldn't be here like this now." She raged in an uncommonly quiet and exasperated tone. Then, as her heart started to race as she suspected what his answer would be based on his behaviour so far, she held up the card Kaelan had given her.

"Please call the hit off. You gain nothing, prevent nothing, by going through with it."

Fists clenched in rage Jonathon shot to his feet and advanced on her, "No! I will not have you tell me want to do..." That was all Jonathon managed to snarl out at her as a number of things happened all at once...

She dropped the card when she let her hand fall to her side the moment he said no and she started to turn to walk away, to meet with her death. She didn't get far as Maria, from behind, wrapped her arms around the young woman in comfort.

Lucidia distanced herself further from her husband, staggering backwards three or so steps in horror at Jonathon's words. Looking at her, Sarah could see the woman had just discovered she didn't really know her husband after all.

The rest of the Lepe physically distanced themselves as well but made sure they could still see any and all that might yet happen.

Antonio's hands changed and he leaped towards Jonathon. As Jonathon used both of his to block Antonio's left hand in the effort to overpower his second in command, it left him open to Antonio's right hand. But not before Jonathon's hands changed and he dug his own claws into Antonio's arm. With a growl of pain, Antonio's right hand claws sunk deep into Jonathon's throat as the second in command extinguished his leader's life by ripping the man's throat out.

As much as she hated such violence, Sarah forced herself to watch the struggle between the two men. She did so because she felt responsible for Antonio being caught in the middle of a situation that was between Jonathon and herself. The other thing she hated in that moment was being up close and personal to the fighting.

Then, just like that, the fight was over. Maria rushed to her husband's side and Sarah stayed where she was. Feeling something warm soaking into the front of her dress, she pulled it away from herself and gazed down at it. The front of her was covered in Jonathon's blood.

'Damn it! I love this dress.' Then she sighed. 'What difference does it make? So his will be included with mine soon.'

With Jonathon's death, so died her only chance to live. Everyone was occupied with the new change in leadership as they gathered around Antonio. No one was looking at her so she turned around and started walking back the way she had come. She was a quarter of the way out of the bushland when Antonio started after her, calling her name. Having since learnt how to keep moving without being seen, she didn't stop. What would be the point? She left Jonathon's home and headed to the paintball range.

*

Other than hurting a few muscles, busting the rowing machine in his frustration and dripping with sweat, the workout failed to distract him. Kaelan went upstairs to have a shower. With a towel around his hips, he wandered through the house. She was everywhere. Not just with her belongings, but with the little touches she had added and her scent. He decided in that moment he would never come back.

'I'll move my weapons to my other home and sell this place, business included. I'd really thought I would have been able to call this place home again when I'd asked her if she would like to move in. She had admitted to not caring about what I do for a living after all. How could I not ask her? I was hoping she might even grow to love me, but it hadn't gone that way after she became therian. Where she's concerned, I've fucked up badly. Mum and Dad would be disappointed if they were still alive.'

He paused for a moment. 'Damn! But I haven't thought about them in years.'

Back in the bedroom he halted by her dressing table. He paused slightly before opening the drawer. Right at the front, on top of everything else was an envelope addressed to him.

'I don't even know when she'd written it.'

His hand hovered over it then he sighed, slammed the drawer shut and got dressed, got in the Jeep and drove off to the paintball range. The night was clear, not a cloud to be seen. It was obscene.

'The night should be miserable for this particular job. Just like the way I feel.'

In some places he could just see the moon rising. It was huge and a bluish yellow as it hung half way to its zenith in sky. 'It must have been a deeper yellow when it was lower. Like that, one can see why it's been called cheese at times.' He didn't even try to censor the trivial thought. Anything was better than thinking about the job at hand. He drove trying not to think of a damned thing other than the traffic around him. The roads were busier than usual.

Half way to his destination, his mobile rang. Even though he had earphones in, he pulled over not wanting the cops stopping him to write him a ticket or anything else. He glanced at the number. Not one of the ones he was expecting but vaguely recognised it. 'Has she been successful after all?'

Even though his heart was pounding away, he managed to answer the phone sounding calm. "Yes?"

He wasn't surprised to hear a man's voice, even if it wasn't the one he was expecting, but was surprised with what the caller had said.

"The hit is cancelled. Please, I'm Antonio and I've just killed Jonathon for his stupidity. I think she knows that he's now dead but I'm not certain. She dropped your card when he refused to cancel the hit. She's now on her way to meet with you, so she doesn't know this call is happening. Please! I beg you, don't kill her. Keep the money since Jonathon doesn't need it anymore. Just don't kill her please." His voice had come out in a rush, not giving Kaelan a chance to say a word until his last pleading petered out.

"Thanks for the money. The hit is now called off. See if you can access the site Sutterton used to initiate the hit and change the status to 'cancelled by contractor' so no one else will take it up." He said tonelessly then hung up before the therian could say anything else.

'While I'm relieved at not having to go through with the hit, I am disappointed at not getting the chance to kill Sutterton myself and that I won't get to come up against her. Then there's the issue of her not being interested in me. I'm back to square one with her, confused and so in love with her I don't know what to do about it.'

With a sigh, he flicked the indicator on and merged back onto the road and continued to the paintball range.

Chapter 17

Sarah didn't think she was in her right mind when she rode to the paintball range, due to not remembering getting there. She didn't remember the traffic, the lights or anything else along the way. Only, she couldn't have been speeding because she didn't remember being pulled over by the police. She was early, Kaelan hadn't arrived yet. Not that she had long to wait.

So, she sat at the table where she first saw him leaning against his Jeep four years ago and waited for him to arrive. For the first time since she saw him, she wished she had died the day her husband had, or the evening her friends had, or the evening she had become a therian. It seemed cruel to have survived those three only to die now because of some power hungry jerk.

Pulling into the paintball range's driveway he could see she was already there, at the table where they had first seen each other. When she saw his jeep arriving, she stood up. He noted she was dressed in the same clothing he had seen her in when she left to meet up with Sutterton, but there was something strange about it that he couldn't put his finger on. However, it proved she had ridden straight to the paintball range from Sutteron's place. By the time he had the Jeep parked – whether deliberate or accidental but he parked where he had been when she had first seen him – she was walking to the field where they had their first paintball game.

'Her walking is a hell of a lot better now than it had been a few years ago when we were last here.'

She didn't wait for him as she walked onto the field and around the derelict building. She could hear him coming up behind her. It wasn't by accident that she chose the clearing, on the far side of the derelict building, where she had first 'killed' him. She also knew he would recognise the spot.

Everything at the range was the same from when he had first seen her. While some of the plants might be larger, nothing had truly changed. However, Kaelan didn't believe it was accidental that Sarah had chosen that particular clearing. He did think it was ironic though.

'It was where she'd first 'killed' me. Now it looks like I'm to truly kill her here.'

She slowly turned towards him, not saying a word. In that moment he saw the dark stain on the front of her dress and knew it had to be Sutterton's blood.

'Yes. She knows he's dead.'

Also not saying a word, he stopped when she stopped and just watched her. He didn't know why he didn't tell her right then about the hit being cancelled, other than maybe to see what she would do since she thought it was still a go-ahead.

The silence between them stretched and they both let it

happen. She wasn't ready to break it and he didn't seem to have any intentions of doing so. With him watching, she peered around the area, noting the light and shadows throughout then peered down at her feet. Both of them noticed that she was striped with shadows and moonlight.

She looked up at him again. In a voice barely above a whisper, she spoke first. "Have you ever seen a therian change outside of a fight situation?"

"No." He said cautiously, ensuring his face revealed nothing. 'Are we going to fight after all? Am I finally going to see how good she really is?' He kept an extremely tight rein on his excitement as he really did want to see her in action.

"The change during a fight is a lot faster, more explosive and violent, than the change when the therian is feeling safe."

'Nothing I hadn't already known other than there's a slower change rate.'

Moving slowly, so as not to get herself shot too soon, she placing her walking stick against the tree next to her, then slipped her shoes off. Next, she slipped her dress then panties off. By some trick of the light and shadows he couldn't see her nakedness. Her chest, hips to upper thighs, and mid shins and lower were obscured by leafy branched shadows.

'At least that's how I see her actions.' He thought as he watched her, keeping his surprise over her undressing in check. Moonlight glinted on bare pale flesh. Regardless of trying to stay neutral, his body reacted to the knowledge of her standing naked in front of him. Despite her being completely naked, he couldn't see it. 'The shadows fall in just the *right* places for her.'

It took a lot of effort to keep his face blank while he just stood there and looked at her because he had wanted to see her like that for ages. He couldn't help himself as his eyes travelled the length of her a number of times. 'She's beautiful and I want to hold her.' However, he didn't because he wanted to see where she was taking the situation. Whether she knew it or not, she was in control of the situation in that moment.

Kaelan stood there, face blank, barely moving and just watched her. She guessed he was just another man who wasn't interested in her after all. Again, that casual dismissal hurt. Somehow, she thought that hurt more than her dying was going to. Attempting to speak, nothing came out so she cleared her throat and tried again.

"I can also change just my hands." She held up her hands into the light, changed one then the other then both together and then let both revert back to normal.

Kaelan's heart started beating so hard and fast in his chest. 'She's a fucking alpha! They're worse in a fight than any other therian, very vicious to come up against because of their ability to change just their hands. There's no warning when they do so. That was one piece of information never included in the reports. Maybe the informants never saw any of the fights. It's the only thing I can think of.'

After a moment's pause she then proceeded to do a full change.

What he would have normally seen at full fighting speed was slowed down. It still happened fairly quickly, but he could still see the changes happening. Her skin stretched then tore; sounding like thick wet fabric, as her bones and muscles moved, contorted and reshaped themselves into their new form with popping and sucking sounds. In the silence around them, the sounds of her change seemed exceptionally loud and painful. Then the fur started flowing. It was the only way to describe it. Through it all she didn't utter a cry of any kind.

'Yes, it is a lot slower than all the ones I'd previously seen. While under other circumstances it might have been interesting to watch, but to see her body go through that and see the pain on her face is something I'm never going to forget.'

Her pale coloured fur flowed from her skin to cover her whole body. To top it off, a tail appeared to be slowly, almost tranquilly, swinging from side to side once it grew from her tailbone. It took a lot of effort not to smile at such a cute tail. Out straight the tip of the tail would brush the ground, however, the tip curled slightly so it didn't touch the ground at all.

If its swishing was anything to go by then she was calm. If she was then that fact surprised him.

She stood there for a moment regaining her equilibrium then she gazed up at him. To him, even though she appeared to be calm it almost looked like she was feeling a little dizzy but he wasn't good at reading therian faces.

'I have to say for a therian she is one hell of a damned cute cat.'

She realised she wasn't really much taller, if at all, compared to her human form.

'It will be an interesting fight.' He mused.

Having a muzzle, she had to speak a little louder and pronounce her words carefully so he could understand her. Her voice was a sort of growling purr that sent shivers up his spine in a surprisingly pleasant way.

"I thought you should see the process slowly at least once in your life. It looks gross but it's still interesting just the same. Also, I thought you should see *me* like this at least once. Just once." She stepped back slightly to rebalance herself.

He just stood there and didn't say a word. Even his expression hadn't changed. In her opinion, he gave away nothing. While he really didn't know what to say, he didn't exactly trust what might come out of his mouth right then.

Then for the first time ever, he got to see the change in reverse on a living therian and, by the expression on her face, it looked like it hurt. A lot. While she realised the enforced change-back hurt more because she hadn't practiced it all that often. So much so, she fell to the ground in human form, panting from the pain and effort.

Kaelan couldn't help noticing how her falling had her draped across herself so she ended up covering herself just right. He started to go to her but forced himself to stop after that one step. It took a lot of effort to not go to her. He couldn't risk it. He just didn't know where all of it was leading.

For once she wanted him to come to her, to help her, to hold her. She sat where she was for a few moments, not only to recover but to regain control of the threatening tears. A moment or so later, she slowly half crawled and half dragged herself over a ground littered with dead leaves, twigs and small loose rocks to the tree where her walking stick and clothing were. It hurt, but she had no choice since he wasn't helping her to her feet this time.

He wanted to go to her to help her but he couldn't. 'It's not just because she's complained in the past about me seeing her naked. If we're going to fight then I can't let my feelings for her interfere with my ability to fight her.'

While still on the ground, she dressed then used the tree to haul herself into a standing position. She leaned against the tree waiting for the effects of the change to ease. Then, she slipped her shoes on and leant on the walking stick once it was in her hand. The changes obviously took a lot out of her.

What he didn't understand was why she had changed back. 'Fighting me would have been easier for her if she had stayed in jag form.' So, he voiced his thoughts.

"Why didn't you stay in that form? It would have been easier for you to attack me." He asked, sounding angry, confused, frustrated. Yes very frustrated.

"You don't understand do you? I'm not here to protect myself Kaelan. That has never been my intention. The hit has been placed and if you don't do it because I've killed you then someone else will and I'm betting it won't be as pleasant if someone else does it. And not just because I'm a therian, but because I would have killed a fellow bounty hunter." She kept her voice low because there was no need to speak louder.

Based on how the system works, he knew she was correct. However, he still didn't understand and, unfortunately, let his frustration show. "You can't *not* fight Sarah."

It was her turn to not understand why he sounded angry, frustrated. He had promised after all.

Suddenly she stormed towards him, pretending to give him the fight he wanted if it would make him feel better at fulfilling his promise. In barely a blink, he had the gun in his hand and aimed at her before she was even close to him. Her momentum took her so far forward that the end of the gun was pressed rather firmly against her forehead.

However, he didn't pull the trigger. That both surprised and angered him. She had given him the chance and he hadn't taken it. Regardless, she herself never attacked him, not even her hands had changed, and that frustrated him as well.

"And yet, you don't pull the trigger Kaelan." She stated softly with the gun still pressed against her head.

She had rolled her eyes up at him and stayed where she was. Even though she was at arm's length, it still had to be a strain to look up at him like that.

'Her voicing my thoughts like that isn't helping me any.' He suddenly took the gun away from her head and she rocked on the spot slightly. Kaelan stormed away from her, towards the building, then turned towards her again and couldn't hide his anger. She saw anger and something else but she didn't understand why he would still be angry over this.

"You're better than you think you are. I know you can fight. I heard about the jag you clawed and the vamp you killed about a month or so ago. Why won't you at least try?!" He raged at her, but in reality he was angry more at himself because he didn't pull the trigger when she had given him the excuse he was after.

'Looks like our last moments together are going to be him angry at me one last time.' That left her more upset than her impending death.

Her sadness was obvious, even in the darkness, and he didn't understand why she should have been regardless of the situation.

"If I wasn't going to die then I might be able to answer that question. However, as it is, it's one I'll never be able to answer for you. To leave you with the answer, then I die, will do you no favours for the rest of your life. That piece of information is useless to you once I'm dead." She said softly, sadly, as he frowned at her response. It was the closest she had gotten to telling him she loved him but she wouldn't, couldn't, torture him that way.

'What sort of crap answer is that?! It makes no fucking sense what-so-ever!' He wanted to shake her and get her to tell him why, but didn't. He knew it wouldn't achieve anything. He just stood where he was. For the first time in his career, he didn't know what to do.

Then ever so slightly, she turned away from him and stared at her feet. "Just do it please. No more stalling... please." She pleaded softly.

Despite everything, he couldn't believe his ears.

'She's just fucking well pleaded for me to do it!' Confusion, anger and frustration whirlpooled within him in regards to her and himself.

'I can't do it. Not because the hit has been cancelled, but because I fucking love her!' He walked away from her. When the building was between them he angrily called out, informing her.

"You're free to go home Sarah. The hit was called off." Pausing slightly he added in a softer tone, thinking she wouldn't hear him from that distance. "God! This would be so much easier if I didn't love you."

He didn't look back as he stormed back to the parking lot. He got in the Jeep and didn't look back. He drove off and still didn't look back. He didn't look back until he had other traffic around him and even then it was a few minutes after that before he used his mirrors to keep an eye on the traffic around him. But to see her one more time?

He never looked back.

Sarah heard footsteps in the dirt, but she wouldn't... couldn't look at him. She knew she should have, it was cowardice on her part. However, when he spoke it was from further away than she was expecting.

"You're free to go home Sarah. The hit was called off." He called out angrily. Then, so quietly that she barely heard it, "God! This would be so much easier if I didn't love you."

'What?!' Not quite believing her ears, she spun around. He was gone.

Ignoring the fact that she didn't understand why he hadn't told her about the cancelled hit earlier than this, she hobbled quickly after him.

"Kaelan, wait." She called out desperately before she could see him since he had a head start on her.

However, she heard the Jeep drive off before she could reach the parking area. She steadied herself against a tree she had stopped beside as the tears started flowing and she cried so hard.

Jerking her right hand upwards, she caught her walking stick by its base. Gripping it like a cricket bat she then swung it savagely at the tree beside her over and over. Ignoring the pain in her hands as its impact with the tree bit into her flesh painfully, she kept swinging until it was nothing but kindling at her feet and other bits that flew off into the darkness.

She bit her bottom lip to stop the scream that was building at the bottom of her throat. Instead, it came out as a high keening sound through her clenched teeth as she cried. She couldn't see what she was doing because tears were flowing thick and fast.

Sarah savagely wiped at the blood from her lip and the tears on her face.

'Why would he say that then just leave without giving me a chance?' Another sob escaped.

'It's over. It's obvious he truly does think of me as a monster. That it's too much for him, as a bounty hunter, to handle living with one. God! I've been deluding myself for years so badly. Well, no more! I quit... I give up... I'm not interested in anyone else and he obviously can't deal with me being what I am.'

With another desolate sounding sob, she grabbed her helmet and gloves, shoved them on and rode off. Where? She didn't know. She didn't care. She just didn't go back home.

Extras

Bio

Back in 1967 KC was born on the morning of a black Monday on the Sunshine Coast north of Brisbane, Queensland, Australia. KC is the first to admit that her life was nothing special. She has worked as mechanic, in a book shop and in an IT company. Her interest in computers led her to do volunteer teaching online within the graphics community. Her internet time also sparked her interest in puzzle based games, graphics and internet communities based around her pastimes. Eventually, her pastimes led to the first in her Unnaturals of Brisbane series. She is an avid reader and a cat lover.

Below are ways to follow KC. While she's slack with posting, she uses her facebook author page as her blog.

http://www.kcrileygyer.com/

https://www.facebook.com/KCRileyGyerAuthorPage

https://www.facebook.com/KCRileyGyer

https://www.amazon.com/Author/kcrileygyer

https://www.goodreads.com/KCRileyGyer

Excerpt

Changes in Choices
Coming soon

Chapter 1

A week later, Sarah finally showed up back home for the first time since that night at the paintball range, and she was sure she looked like crap! She knew she felt like it. Her dress was dirty with the hem shredded in various spots, her hair unwashed and she smelled. She hadn't really cared at the time because she had stayed away from people so no one saw her. If anyone asked her how she got home she wouldn't be able to answer because she didn't know how she had managed it.

However, she didn't even get the chance to get off the scooter before a set of hands grabbed at her arms roughly, savagely pulling her off the scooter.

"Where the fuck have you been Sarah?! We've been so worried, we thought you were dead." Toby yelled at her, his face red with anger.

She just stood there as his grip bruised her arms, letting him stare at her helmeted head as it wobbled on her neck as he shook her. Mick gently placed a hand on Toby's arm. Toby frowned at him. Mick shook his head then Toby let her go with a slight shove so she staggered back a step then rocked on the spot.

Standing there for just a moment she then reached up to take off her helmet. She didn't look at them and didn't make any move towards the house.

"Geez Sarah! What have you been doing?" Mick exclaimed softly. While he knew her dress was a mess, he wasn't expecting the sight of her face and hair. Her hair was matted and her farce dirty with dark circles under her eyes like someone had used her as a punching bag. Suddenly he scooped her up into his arms and headed towards the house. The helmet dropped from her hand as he lifted her. "Toby, grab her walking stick and helmet please."

After a few moments, "Sarah, where's your stick?" Toby demanded.

"Gone." She answered softly and tonelessly as her head rested on Mick's shoulder.

"What do you mean 'gone'?!" Toby demanded angrily as Mick took her upstairs, but she didn't respond.

Mick sat Sarah at the kitchen table, made her a cup of tea and set it in front of her. She just stared at the table with her hands in my lap. "Drink your tea Sarah." Mick encouraged.

She just sat there not moving, staring at nothing.

Mick was becoming worried. 'Sure she had withdrawn before a number of times but never like this.'

"What's wrong with you Sarah?" Toby asked. Even in her current state she could hear the frown in his voice.

"Nothing." She responded in the same tone of voice as before.

Toby threw up his hands in frustration. "I give up. Fine, be that way. We don't hear from you for a week after Antonio told us about the hit Jonathon took out against you and that you said you had organised such a situation with a friend to complete the hit if it should happen. Was it Kaelan...?" He paused after snarling the other man's name, shook his head and made a sound of frustration before continuing, "Fuck Sarah! With no thought about us being worried about you, you then just rock up like nothing is wrong and you think we don't deserve an explanation of any kind. There are times when you are a selfish bitch and this is one of them, Sarah."

"I'm sorry." While the response was automatic she did mean it but still toneless. She couldn't do what he wanted. Tears weren't even welling up.

Mick placed his hand on Toby's arm again, giving it a gentle tug. Seemed her peripheral vision was still working just fine as her brain registered what she saw. Mick pulled Toby to one side and spoke quietly to Toby, and she discovered that her hearing was working fine as well.

"Look at her. If I didn't know any better I would say she's in shock. She has never let herself look like that ever during the couple of years we've known her. She's just sitting there and hasn't even blinked. Something happened and it hasn't had a good effect on her."

Toby spoke just as quietly after a few moments pause. "Ah shit. I was so angry and concerned about her that I didn't really look at her. Go run a bath so we can clean her up and we'll put her to bed."

They were almost whispering but she could still hear them.

"Okay." Then Mick walked away.

"Come on Sarah, let's get you cleaned up." Toby said gently.

She sat there. Not out of stubbornness but because she was

having a difficult time remembering how to do what he wanted her to do. Toby gently grabbed her, turned her sideways on the seat then stood her up and still she didn't move. He picked her up in his arms and took her to the bathroom. Noting how she just laid limply in his arm, he knew without a doubt that Mick was right. Since it was obvious that Kaelan, or whoever, didn't go through with the hit he wondered what the hell had happened to leave her in such a state.

Toby set Sarah on her feet and proceeded to undress her. Something in her mind was trying to tell her something but she couldn't hear it for the thick fog that was clogging the inside of her mind. Toby then lifted her again and placed her in the hot water.

She laid there staring ahead, then slowly limb by limb the heat of the water soaked in and her body started to relax and her eyes closed.

www.ingramcontent.com/pod-product-compliance
Lightning Source LLC
Chambersburg PA
CBHW070904180626
46817CB00003B/906